NORSE
MYTHS

NORSE MYTHS

MAGICAL TALES OF THE GODS OF ASGARD

JANE SMITHSON

SIRIUS

SIRIUS

This edition published in 2024 by Sirius Publishing, a division of
Arcturus Publishing Limited,
26/27 Bickels Yard, 151–153 Bermondsey Street,
London SE1 3HA

ISBN: 978-1-3988-4326-4
AD011898UK

Printed in China

CONTENTS

Introduction

Norse mythology is the body of myths belonging to the peoples of northern Europe and more specifically Scandinavia. Many arose from Old Norse religion, but continued after the Scandinavians embraced Christianity, and fed into the Nordic folklore of the modern period. Norse myths are considered the northernmost extension of Germanic mythology and consist of tales of various deities, beings, and heroes. Derived from numerous sources from the pagan period and earlier, including medieval manuscripts, archaeological representations, and folk tradition, the source texts include deities such as Thor, the god of thunder, Odin, flanked by his ravens, the goddess Freya, with her chariot drawn by cats, along with many other gods.

Much of the Norse mythology that survives is based around the plight of the gods and their relationships with other beings, some of them humans as well the *jötnar*, beings who may be friends, lovers, foes, or family members of the gods. In Norse mythology a sacred tree, *Yggdrasil* is the centre of the cosmos, surrounded by the 'nine worlds'. Certain units of time and elements of the cosmology are personified as deities or other beings.

Most of the Norse mythology we know today is drawn from two sources. The Eddas are two Icelandic literary works, a collection of poems and a prose work, both containing many stories. The Sagas are various prose stories and histories, originating in Iceland and elsewhere in Scandinavia.

The tales recounted here are drawn from both sources and contain many of the best known legends from Norse mythology including how Odin sought for wisdom, how Thor gained his hammer – and his many trials, the story of why the Fenris Wolf was bound, as well as, threaded through several of the stories, and the activities of Loki, the trickster god, who eventually gets his comeuppance.

Thrilling and elemental, the stories reach right back to the very founding of the world and tell of lands of fire and ice and the gods and men who try to contain them.

The Beginning

In the beginning, when the beautiful and sunny world was first made, there stood, in the very midst of all its beauty, Mount Ida – a mountain so high, so far away up among the snowy clouds, that its summit was lost in the shining light of the rays of the sun.

At its base, stretching away to the north, the south, the east, and the west, as far as even the eyes of the gods could reach, lay the soft, green valleys and the great, broad plain beyond. Encircling the whole great plain, and curling lovingly around in all the little bends and bays of the distant shore, lay the deep blue waters; and beyond the waters, hidden in the distant mists, rose the great mountains in which the frost giants dwelt.

On the top of Mount Ida, the gods had built their shining city, Asgard; and from its golden gateway to the valley below was stretched the richly coloured, rainbow bridge, with its wonderful bars of red and yellow and blue, orange and green, indigo and purple.

And in this shining city, where the gods dwelt, there was no sorrow, no grief, no pain of any kind. Never was the sun's

light shut off by heavy clouds; never did the cruel lightnings flash, nor came their blights upon the harvest fields; never did the heavy rains fall, nor did the cold winds sweep down upon this shining city.

But alas, there came a time when a shadow fell upon this city that shone so like a golden cloud resting upon the mountain peak. For the Fates, the three cruel sisters, came and took up their abode at the foot of the wonderful tree of Life, whose roots were in the earth, and whose branches, reaching high above the shining city, protected it from the sun's fierce heat and strong white light. And from that time even the gods themselves were no longer free from care and sorrow.

Envy sprang up among the children of the great god, Odin; sickness, and even death, fell upon them; and the frost giants waged war with them – a war that would never cease in all the ages that were to come, until that day when the sun's light went out forever, and the dark reign of Ragnarök fell upon the earth.

It was a beautiful earth that lay stretched out at the foot of Mount Ida. The fields were rich with grain; the trees were loaded with fruits; the sun shone warm and bright; but there were no harvesters, no gatherers of the fruit, no children to run and frolic in the sunshine.

"The fair earth is desolate," said Odin to himself, as he looked down from his golden temple. "There should be people there, not gods and goddesses like us here upon Mount Ida, but beings less powerful than we, beings who can love and enjoy, and whose children shall fill the earth with their happy voices. And the care of all these beings shall be mine."

As he spoke, he, the All-Father, passed down the rainbow bridge, out into the rich, green valley below.

As he passed on beneath the trees, he saw standing together, their branches bending towards each other, a straight, strong Ash and a gentle, graceful Elm.

"From these trees," said Odin to himself, "will I create the earth-people. The man I will name Ask, and the woman, Embla. It is a beautiful, sunny world: they should be very happy in it. How their children shall delight in the broad fields and the sunny slopes! And no harm shall come to them; for I, the All-Father, will watch over them in all the ages to come."

The Well of Wisdom

One night when all was quiet in Asgard and the Aesir had gone to rest, Odin, the All-father, sat awake on his high throne, troubled with many thoughts. At his feet crouched his two faithful wolves, and upon his shoulders perched the two ravens of thought and memory, who flew far abroad every day, through the nine worlds, as Odin's messengers.

The All-father had need of great wisdom in ruling the worlds; after thinking a long time on the matters which needed his care, he suddenly started up, and went forth with long strides from his palace of Gladsheim into the night. He soon returned, leading his beautiful, eight-footed steed, Sleipnir, and it was plain that Odin was going on a journey. He quickly mounted Sleipnir, and rode swiftly away toward Bifröst, the rainbow bridge, which reached from Asgard, the city of the gods, down through the air to the lower worlds.

When Sleipnir stepped upon the bridge it trembled, and seemed hardly strong enough to bear the horse and his rider; but they had no fear of its giving way, and Sleipnir galloped swiftly onward.

Soon Odin saw Heimdall, the watchman of the bridge, riding toward him on a fine horse, with a golden mane that reflected light upon the noble face of his rider.

"You must be bound on some important errand, Father Odin, to be riding forth from Asgard so late at night," said Heimdall.

"It is indeed a most important errand, and I must hasten on," replied Odin. "It is well for us that we have such a faithful guardian of the 'trembling bridge'; if it were not for you, Heimdall, our enemies might long ago have taken Asgard by storm. You are so watchful, you can hear the grass grow in the fields, and the wool gather on the backs of the sheep, and you need less sleep than a bird. I myself stand in great need of wisdom, in order to take care of such faithful servants, and to drive back such wicked enemies!"

They hurried over the bridge until they came to Heimdall's far-shining castle, at the farther end of it. This was a lofty tower which was placed so as to guard the bridge, and it sent forth into the land of the giant enemies such a wonderful, clear light, that Heimdall could see, even in the darkest night, any one who came toward the bridge. Here Odin stopped a few moments to drink the mead which the good Heimdall offered him.

Then said Odin, "As I am journeying into the land of our enemies, I shall leave my good horse with you; there are not many with whom I would trust him, but I know that you, my faithful Heimdall, will take good care of him. I can best hide myself from the giants by going on as a wanderer."

With these words the Allfather quitted Heimdall's castle, and started off toward the north, through the land of the fierce giants.

During all the first day there was nothing to be seen but ice and snow; several times Odin was nearly crushed as the frost giants hurled huge blocks of ice after him.

The second day he came to mountains and broad rivers. Often when he had just crossed over a stream, the mountain giants would come after him to the other bank, and when they found that Odin had escaped them, they would send forth such a fierce yell, that the echoes sounded from hill to hill.

At the end of the third day, Odin came to a land where trees were green and flowers blooming. Here was one of the three fountains which watered the world tree, Yggdrasil, and near by sat the wise giant, Mimir, guarding the waters of this wonderful fountain, for whoever drank of it would have the gift of great wisdom.

Mimir was a giant in size, but he was not one of the fierce giant enemies of the gods, for he was kind, and wiser than the wisest.

Mimir's well of wisdom was in the midst of a wonderful valley, filled with rare plants and bright flowers, and among the groves of beautiful trees were strange creatures, sleeping dragons, harmless serpents, and lizards, while birds with gay plumage flew and sang among the branches. Over all this quiet valley shone a lovely soft light, different from sunlight, and in the centre grew one of the roots of the great world tree. Here the wise giant Mimir sat gazing down into his well.

Odin greeted the kind old giant, and said, "Oh, Mimir, I have come from far-away Asgard to ask a great boon!"

"Gladly will I help you if it is in my power," said Mimir.

"You know," replied Odin, "that as father of gods and men I need great wisdom, and I have come to beg for one drink of

your precious water of knowledge. Trouble threatens us, even from one of the Aesir, for Loki, the fire-god, has lately been visiting the giants, and I fear he has been learning evil ways from them. The frost giants and the storm giants are always at work, trying to overthrow both gods and men; great is my need of wisdom, and even though no one ever before has dared ask so great a gift, I hope that since you know how deep is my trouble, you will grant my request."

Mimir sat silently, thinking for several moments, and then said, "You ask a great thing, indeed, Father Odin; are you ready to pay the price which I must demand?"

"Yes," said Odin, cheerfully, "I will give you all the gold and silver of Asgard, and all the jewelled shields and swords of the Aesir. More than all, I will give up my eight-footed horse Sleipnir, if that is needed to win the reward."

"And do you suppose that these things will buy wisdom?" said Mimir.

"That can be gained only by bearing bravely, and giving up to others. Are you willing to give me a part of yourself? Will you give up one of your own eyes?"

At this Odin looked very sad; but after a few moments of deep thought, he looked up with a bright smile, and answered, "Yes, I will even give you one of my eyes, and I will suffer whatever else is asked, in order to gain the wisdom that I need!"

We cannot know all that Odin bravely suffered in that strange, bright valley, before he was rewarded with a drink from that wonderful fountain; but we may be quite sure that never once was the good All-father sorry for anything he had given up, or any suffering he had borne, for the sake of others.

The Stolen Wine

There had lain for ages upon ages, hidden away in the great rocky cellar of one of the giant's castles, a cask of wine, which had been stolen from the gods.

Never before had the gods been able to learn what had become of it; what giant had stolen it, nor in what castle it was hidden.

But now that Odin had become All-wise, nothing could be concealed from him.

"I know at last where the wine lies hidden," said Odin one day to his son, Thor; "and I shall set forth to find it."

Thor brought down his hammer with a thud. "Let me go with you," cried he, springing up. "And let me fell to the earth with one blow of my magic hammer the giant who has stolen, and has kept hidden all these ages our precious wine."

"No;" answered Odin, "this time I must go alone. The wine is guarded day and night, and it will not be easy to bring it away, even when I have found it. But watch for me, dear son. One day there will come, beating its wings against the shining gates of our city, a great white eagle. Do not harm the eagle. Open the gates to him; for that eagle will be Odin, returning with the stolen wine to our city of Asgard."

Then Odin put aside his sparkling crown and laid down his sceptre. His wonderful blue mantle, studded with stars and fastened always with a pale crescent moon, he also threw aside, and stepped forth in the garb of a common labourer. "It is in this guise that I shall win my way to the giant's castle," said Odin; and in a second he had passed out from the hall and was gone.

It was the giant, Suttung, that had stolen the wine, and it was in his castle that it had lain hidden all these years.

Now, of all the strong castles of all the giants, Suttung's castle was the strongest. The cellar was cut into the solid rock. Moreover, three sides of the castle rose in solid walls of granite; while the fourth, no less firm and strong, was built of massive blocks bound with hoops and bars and bolts of strongest iron and steel.

Now, Suttung had a brother, Bauge, who was a giant farmer. He kept nine strong slaves, half giants themselves, to do his work for him.

As Odin approached the fields of Bauge's farm, he saw the nine men hard at work.

"Your scythes are dull," said he, as he drew near.

"Yes, but we have no whetstone to sharpen them upon," answered the workmen, the great drops standing out upon their foreheads.

"I will sharpen them on mine," said Odin, drawing one from his pocket.

"It is a magic whetstone!" cried the men as they saw it

work. "Give it to us. We need it more than you. Give it to us. Give it to us."

"Take it, then," answered Odin, throwing it high in the air and walking off.

"It is mine! It is mine! Let me have it! Give it to me! I will have it! Out of the way! It shall be mine!" screamed and quarrelled the nine men as they pushed and crowded, each one determined to catch the whetstone as it came down to earth.

At last it fell. Then a fiercer battle followed. The angry men fell upon each other. They dragged and pulled and threw each other to the ground. They pounded each other; they struck at each other with their scythes. On and on they fought. Hour after hour the battle waged; till at last the Sun-god, in sheer dismay at so unloving a sight, hid his face behind the hills, and the nine men lay dead upon the fields.

It was an hour later when Odin reached the castle of Bauge.

"Can you give me shelter for the night?" he asked, as the giant appeared at the door of his castle.

"Yes, I can give you shelter; but you must look elsewhere for your breakfast. A strange thing has happened. My nine slaves, while at work in the field, have fallen in battle upon

each other, and have killed each other. Not one of them is left alive to serve me."

"They must have been idle, quarrelsome fellows," answered Odin.

"They were, indeed," answered Bauge; "but how shall I get my work done without them?"

"I will do the work for you," answered Odin.

"You! There is but one of you, even if you were willing to try," answered Bauge with but little interest.

"But I can do the work of any nine workmen that ever served you."

The giant laughed. "A remarkable workman. Pray, do you ask the wages of nine men as well?"

"I ask no wages," answered Odin. "I only ask that, as my pay when the work is done, you shall give me a draught of wine from the cask hidden in your brother's cellar."

Bauge stared. "How did you know there is a cask in my brother's cellar?" he gasped.

"It is enough that I know it," answered Odin coldly.

Bauge looked at Odin. "He is better than no man," he thought to himself. "I may as well get what work from him I can, before he finds that no being on earth can enter that cellar or force my brother to give away one drop of that wine."

"Very well, you may go to work," he said aloud. "I cannot promise you that we can make our way into my brother's cellar; but I will do what I can to help you."

"That is all I ask," answered Odin. "Now let me sleep, for I am tired; and if I am to do nine men's work, I must have nine men's sleep."

"And must you have nine men's food?" cried Bauge.

"I think it very likely," answered Odin with a queer smile. "Now let me sleep."

* * *

"What is your name?" asked Bauge of his new workman when they set forth the next morning to the fields.

"You may call me Bolverk," answered Odin.

"Will one name be enough for all nine of you?" said Bauge with a disagreeable curling of his upper lip.

"I will not burden your giant mind with more than one," Odin answered, a funny little twinkle in his eye.

The giant gave a furious grunt. He did not quite know whether his new workman was stupid, or, whether under all his seeming meekness, it might not be that he was making fun of him.

Well, Bauge set Bolverk to work, and then, lazy fellow that he was, stretched himself out on a mountain side to watch.

"That new workman of mine," he bellowed, calling the attention of a neighbour giant to Odin at work in the field;

"do you see him down there among the corn? He says he can do nine men's work."

"A workman usually thinks himself equal to any nine other workingmen," roared back the neighbour. "Of course you have agreed to give him nine men's wages?"

Then the two giants roared with laughter. They thought they had said a very bright thing, and very likely they had. It is only because you and I are mere earth-children that we do not think so too.

As the days went on, Bauge began to laugh less and to wonder more at his strange workman. He worked on quietly from sunrise till sunset. He did not seem to hurry in his work;

he did not work over hours. But, strange to say, the work went on, as the workman had promised. No nine men could have done more or could have done it better.

It was harvest time when Odin came; the time when Frey, the god of the fields and of all that grows, glides around among his children and covers them over, or gathers in their wealth and beauty. Like the kind, loving father he is, he whispers to them now of Njord who so soon will come, sweeping across the earth, breathing his cold freezing breath upon all the world, and covering it over with the cold white sheet that kills the flowers and the fruits. He teaches his children to curl themselves up beneath the earth until the cruel Njord is gone. For Njord seeks to kill the tiny leaves and buds, and shrivel the radiant flowers, that, through all the long warm summer days, have lifted their faces so brightly to their good friend, the Sun-god.

Perhaps it was because Frey and Odin worked together that there were such rare crops, and that the harvesting went on so smoothly. Certain it was that all the fields were cleared, the cellars were filled, and all was ready for the long, cold months to come, when cruel Njord was king.

Even Bauge was in good humour. "You are indeed a wonderful workman," he said to Odin, as the last cellar was fastened and he sat down to rest.

"You are kind," answered Odin, the funny little twinkle coming again into his eyes. "Perhaps you would be willing to come with me now to your brother, that I may drink from the cask of wine that he keeps so closely guarded in his cellar."

Bauge began to feel uncomfortable. "He will not allow either you or me to so much as look upon that wine. You cannot have it."

"Bauge," said Odin, growing very tall and godlike, his wonderful eyes flashing with a light like fire, "you promised to do all you could to help me. Come and do as I bid you."

Bauge stared. His first thought was to kill the workman on the spot: but there was something about him, he hardly knew what, that made him, instead, rise and follow Odin to the brother's castle.

"Tell me which cellar holds the wine," said Odin when they had reached the brother's mountain.

"This one," answered Bauge.

"Now take this augur. Make a hole with it through the solid wall."

Bauge obeyed like one in a dream. It was a magic augur. How it worked! How the powdered stone flew in a cloud about his face!

"This is a very – " Bauge stopped. What had become of his workman? Not a soul was in sight. Odin had disappeared. And to this day the giant never knew what became of him, nor does his brother know who stole his wine from the cellar.

The stupid Bauge stood staring, now at the augur, now at the hole in the wall. He saw a little worm climb up the wall and disappear through the hole. That is all he ever saw or ever knew.

The little worm laughed to itself as it crept in out of sight. "You are very stupid, Bauge, not to know me."

Reaching the inner side of the wall, the little worm stopped to look about. There stood the cask; and beside it sat the daughter of the giant. "Poor girl," said Odin – I mean, said the worm – to himself. "It is a bitter fate to be doomed to sit forever in this wretched dungeon watching your father's stolen treasure. But be happy. Soon you will be free. There will be no wine to watch."

The young giantess must have heard his words. For she looked up. There, just in front of the hole, the ray of light falling full upon his golden hair, stood a most beautiful youth. He looked so kindly upon her, and his eyes were so full of pity!

Her heart went out to him at once.

"I am very tired," said he gently. "So very tired. I have come a long, long distance. My home is far from here. I cannot tell you how far – but very, very far. If you would give me just one draught from the cask of wine."

The poor girl, grateful for the sound of a friendly voice, and for the sight of a human face, arose and lifted the lid for him.

Odin leaned over the cask. He put his lips to the wine and drank.

"You are very thirsty," said the giantess.

"Very," answered Odin, drinking on and on.

"You are very thirsty," said the giantess again.

"Very," answered Odin, still drinking on and on and on.

"You are very thirsty," said the giantess again; this time louder, her voice filled with fear.

"Very," answered Odin, still drinking on and on and on and on. Nor did he stop till every drop was gone and the cask stood dry and empty.

The young giantess, realizing all too late that the wine was stolen, ran to the cellar gateway, shouting as only a giant can shout for help.

The gateway flew open. In rushed the giants, Bauge and his brother.

"The wine! the wine!" they cried.

"Stolen, stolen!" sobbed the giantess, her sobs shaking even the solid cellar walls.

"The thief! The thief!" cried the giants. "Where is the thief?"

But there was no thief to be found. There stood the empty cask. But the thief? There was no living creature to be seen.

No living creature? I should not have said quite that. For there arose from a darkened corner of the cellar a beautiful, great white bird. Its wings brushed against the sides of the gateway as it passed. Then higher and higher, up, up, far, far away beyond the sea, above the clouds it soared, nor rested till its great wings beat against the golden bars of the shining gates of Asgard.

The Hammer of Thor

Thor was the son of Odin. He was a brave young god; and when the frost giants came sweeping down upon the shining city, none were more brave to fight for the protection of Asgard, the beautiful home of the gods, than Thor, the son of Odin.

There was another son, Loki. A cruel, wicked, idle, evil-hearted god was he, the sorrow of his father Odin, the grief of his mother Frigg, and the terror of all the gods and goddesses.

Over this son the great Odin wept often bitter tears. More bitter still since he had drunk from the Well of Wisdom; for since then knowing, as he did, all things past and future, he knew that a day was yet to come, when, because of this wicked Loki, the light would go out from the earth; damp and cold and darkness would fall upon the shining city; the frost giants would overcome the gods; and there would come an end to all life. Nor was there any escape nor hope for any help. This

fate, the Norns had decreed should be; and through the evil-hearted Loki it was to come.

In the golden hall of the gods dwelt Thor; and with him, his beautiful wife, Sif. Of all the goddesses there was none like her. Her eyes were of heaven's own blue; and the light in them was borrowed from the stars. Her hair was of yellow, yellow gold; and as it lay massed above her pure white brow, it vied with the golden light of harvest time in softness and rich, deep colour.

One happy peaceful day, when there was no danger abroad, and rest and peace had spread themselves above the halls of the city of Asgard, Sif lay sleeping. The Sun-god's covering of soft warm rays fell upon her, and the leaves of Yggdrasil had spread themselves above her in tender, loving protection.

Loki, the idle one, angry and revengeful, as he always was, when happiness and rest and peace had driven out sorrow and care, paced angrily up and down the golden streets, his deep black frowns darkening even the clear, white light of heaven.

He came upon the beautiful sleeping wife of Thor.

"I hate my brother," he hissed through his cruel teeth. "And how proud he is of this golden hair of Sif's."

The wicked light flashed from his deep black eyes. Softly, like a thief, he crept towards the sleeping Sif. He seized the golden hair in his hand. A cruel smile shone over his evil face. "Boast now of your beauty, O Sif," he sneered. "Boast now of your Sif's golden hair, O Thor," he growled. And with one great sweep of his shining knife, he cut from the beautiful head the whole mass of gold.

It was late when Sif awoke. The leaves of Yggdrasil were moaning for the cruel deed. The Sun was sinking sorrowfully below the distant mountain peaks.

"O my gold! my gold!" sobbed Sif. "O who has stolen from me in my sleep my gold? O Thor, Thor! You were so proud of the gold. It was for you I prized it – my beautiful, beautiful gold!"

At that second the voice of Thor was heard. His heavy call echoed across the skies and pealed from cloud to cloud. He was angry; for he had heard Sif's bitter cry and felt some harm had come to her.

"It is Loki that has done this," he thundered; and again his voice rolled from cloud to cloud. The very mountain peaks across the sea in the country of the Frost giants rocked and reeled. The waters foamed and tossed; the scorching lightnings flashed from his eyes; the whole sky was as one great sheet of fire.

The earth-children trembled as they had never trembled before. Even Loki, shivering with fear, cowered behind the golden pillars of the great arched gateway.

"Forgive me, forgive me!" wailed he, as Thor flashed his great white light upon him.

"Out from your hiding place, O coward! Out! Out, or my thunderbolts shall strike you dead."

"Spare me, spare me!" groaned Loki. "Only spare me, and I will go down into the earth where the dwarfs do dwell –"

"Go!" thundered Thor, not waiting for the wretched god to finish. "Go, and bring back to me a crown of golden threads, woven and spun in the smithies of the dwarfs, that shall be as beautiful, and ten thousand times more beautiful, than the golden crown you have stolen from the head of Sif. Go to them, tell them what you have done, and never again enter the shining gateway of the city of our Father Odin until you bring the crown."

Loki slunk away, the thunders of the wrath of Thor slowly, slowly following him. The lightnings flashed dully across the skies. The low rumbling of thunder, distant but threatening,

warned Loki that the wrath of Thor was not appeased, neither would it be, nor would there be any return to Asgard for the evil doer, until the crown of gold was won.

* * *

It was away down in the underground caves, and beneath the roaring waters of the rivers, and deep in the hearts of the mountains that these dwarf workmen dwelt, and worked their smithies, and spun their gold and brass.

"Make me a crown of gold for Sif the wife of Thor," snarled Loki, bursting in upon the workshop of the dwarfs.

The dwarfs were ugly little creatures, with crooked legs, and crooked backs. Their eyes were black, wicked little beads of eyes, and their hearts were malicious and sometimes cruel. But they were the willing and ready slaves of the gods; and so, at even this ill-natured command from Loki, they set themselves to work.

The coals burned and blazed; the forges puffed and blew; the little workmen moulded and turned and spun their gold. Hardly had the Sun-god lifted his head above the castles of the frost giants, hardly had his light fallen upon the rich colours of the rainbow bridge, when Loki came forth from the underground caves, the shining crown in his hand.

Quickly he rose high in the air and stood before the gates of the city.

"Have you brought the crown?" thundered Thor from within the gates.

"I have brought the crown," answered Loki in triumph. "And more than that," added he, when the gates had been opened to him, "I have brought as gifts from the dwarfs, a ship that will sail on land or sea and a spear that never fails.

O there are no such workmen among any dwarfs as these who made the spear, the ship and the crown."

"You boast of what you do not know," croaked Brok, a little dwarf who stood near by.

"Who says I do not know?" cried Loki, turning sharply.

"I say you do not know," croaked the little dwarf again, his beadlike eyes snapping angrily, his whole crooked frame quivering with rage. "I have a brother, a workman in brass

and gold, who can make gifts more pleasing to the gods than any you have brought."

Loki looked down upon the little dwarf in scorn. "Go to your brother," he sneered, "and bring to us the wonderful things you think he can make. Bring us one gift more wonderful than these I have, or more acceptable to Odin and Thor, and I will give your brother my head to pay him for his efforts." Then Loki roared with laughter, believing that he had made a rare, rich joke.

Hardly had the roars of laughter died away, when Brok,

gliding down the rainbow bridge with a swiftness equalled only by the lightning, sprang into Midgard, and was making his way towards the great mountain, beneath which worked the forges of his brother, the master-workman – Sindre.

"Some one cometh," said the dwarfs, pausing in their work to listen, their busy hammers in mid-air.

"Fear not," answered Brok, his harsh voice echoing down the great halls. "It is I – Brok – and I come to demand of you that now, if never again, you do your best; for Loki boasts to the gods of Asgard that no dwarfs in all the caverns of the under world can make one gift more wonderful or more acceptable to Odin than those he brings – a crown of gold, a ship that will sail on land or sea, and a spear that never fails!"

A terrible roar burst forth from the hosts of angry dwarfs. "We will see! We will see!" they thundered. And seizing their hammers they set to work. The great forges blazed. The sparks flew. The smoke poured forth from the mountain top. Loki, looking out from the shining city, trembled. Well did he know the workmanship of these dwarfs of Brok; and well did he know how rash had been his scornful promise to the angry little dwarf.

"We will make a hammer for Thor," said Sindre, the greatest among the workmen in this under world; "a hammer, that when thrown from his mighty hand, shall ring through all the heavens. A trail of fire shall follow it. Its aim shall never fail; and it shall carry death and destruction wherever it falls.

"Blow thou the bellows, Brok; and I myself will mould the hammer from the red hot iron."

With Brok at the bellows, the very mountain rocked, and Midgard for miles about was ablaze with the burst of light from the mountain top.

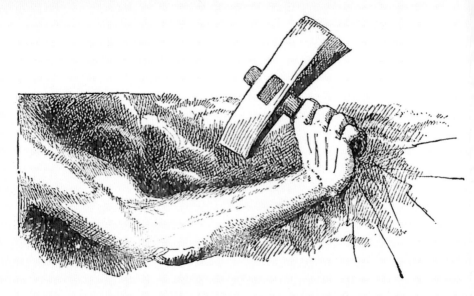

"This shall not be," snarled Loki. And rushing down from Asgard he crouched outside the great, black cave to listen.

"A hammer for Thor!" Those were the words he heard. The ugly face grew uglier. An instant, and there was no Loki at the cavern mouth; but instead, a poisonous, stinging gadfly, whose green back glistened, and whose shining wings buzzed and hummed with cruelty and revenge. There was a hard, ringing tone of defiance in their singing, and the tone was like that of the voice of Loki himself.

"You shall drop the bellows," buzzed the gadfly bitterly, as it alighted upon the neck of Brok.

It was a cruel sting; and its poison forced, even from the sturdy Brok, a cry of pain.

"I know you. It is Loki," he cried; "but I will not drop the bellows though you sting me through and through and with a thousand stings!"

The gadfly buzzed with rage. Straight towards the hand upon the bellows it darted. Brok groaned again. His face grew pale; he quivered with the pain; still he held the mighty bellows and worked the roaring forge.

"You will not!" hissed the gadfly; and again it drove its poison sting, this time straight between the eyes of the suffering dwarf. And now Brok staggered. His hands relaxed their hold. Blinded with pain, he dropped the bellows. The blood ran down his face. The gadfly still hummed and buzzed.

"You have nearly spoiled it," cried Sindre. "Why did you drop the bellows? See how short the handle is! And how rough! But it cannot be helped now; nor will its terror be any less to Loki. Ha, ha, I would have made it handsome; but there is a power in it that shall make even the gods tremble in all the ages to come. Hurry away with it, and place it in Thor's mighty hands. And here are other gifts. Take them all, and bring me Loki's head. He has promised. Surely even he must keep his word, wicked and deceitful though he is."

Brok seized the hammer, and, with the gifts, hurried up through the dark cavern, out into the light of Midgard, up the rainbow bridge, and, with triumph in his swarthy face, sprang into the presence of the great god Odin.

Loki roared with laughter at the sight of the awkward, clumsy hammer; but there was a proud, confident look in the dwarf's shining eyes that Loki did not like; and, coward that he was, his heart began already to fail him.

"Let us see the gifts," said Odin, "that we may judge which workman among the dwarfs has proved himself most wonderful."

"First of all," said Loki, coming forward, "here is the golden crown for Sif."

Eagerly Thor seized the crown, and placed it upon poor Sif's head.

"Wonderful! wonderful!" cried all the gods, for straightway the golden hair began to grow to Sif's head, and in a second it was as if her golden locks had never been stolen from her.

"To you, O Odin," said the dwarf, now coming forward, "I give this ring of gold. It is a magic ring; and each night it

will cast off from itself another ring, as pure and as heavy, as round and as large as itself."

"What is that," sneered Loki, "compared with this? See, O Father Odin, I bring you a magic spear. Accept this, my second gift. It is a magic spear that never fails."

"But behold my second gift," interrupted Brok. "It is a boar of wonderful strength. It, too, is magic. No horse can run, no bird can fly with such speed. It travels both on land and sea; and in the night its bristles shine with such a light, that it matters not how dense the blackness, the forest or the plain will be as bright as noonday."

"I, too, have a gift that will travel on land or sea," cried Loki, pushing himself forward again. "See, it is a ship. And not only will it travel on land or sea, but it can lift itself and sail like a bird above the clouds and through the air."

"It will be hard indeed to say which gift is greatest," said Odin kindly.

"Look now, O, Odin, and Frigg and Thor and Sif and all the gods, at this the last of my three gifts. This hammer, O Thor, I bring to you, the god of thunder. Strike with it, and your thunders shall echo and re-echo from cloud to cloud as never they were heard before. Thrown into the air or at a foe, like Loki's spear, it shall never miss its aim; but, more than that, it shall return always to the hand of Thor. No foe can conceal it, no foe can destroy it. It will never fail thee, O Thor, thou god of thunder."

"But what a clumsy handle," sneered Loki, who already began to fear the hammer was to win the favour of the gods.

"Yes," answered Brok, "the handle is clumsy and it is short. But none knows better than you why it is so."

Loki coloured and moved uneasily. "Do not think," continued Brok, "that I do not know it was you who sent the poisonous gadfly to sting and bite me as I worked at the blazing forge, pounding out the brass and gold from which this hammer is made.

"You thought to pain me into giving up this contest, you coward! you evil one! you boaster!

"When the handle was welded just so far, you drove the gadfly into my eye. I could not see to finish the work; but although the handle is short and clumsy, the magic power is there, and with it in his hand, no power in earth or among the frost giants even can overcome our great god Thor."

A ringing shout of joy arose from the gods. Thor swung his hammer over his head and threw it far out against the clouds. The thunder rolled, the clouds filled with blackness, and the lightnings flashed, as the magic hammer, humming through the air, came back to the hands of Thor.

"Now give me my wager," cried Brok. "I was promised the head of Loki."

"Take it," laughed Loki. "Take it."

Brok drew near. "I will take it," he hissed through his set teeth; "and a rich day will it be both in Midgard and in Asgard when your miserable head is bound down in the home of the dwarfs of the underground world."

"But halt," commanded Loki. "My head you may have; but you must not touch my neck. One drop of blood from that, and you forfeit your life."

Brok stood for a moment white with anger. He knew that he was foiled. Then springing forward, he thundered, "I may not touch your neck; but see, I have my revenge." And so, falling upon Loki, who struggled, but struggled in vain, he whipped from his mantle a thong and thread of brass; and before even Loki knew what had been done, he had sewed, firm together, the lying, boasting lips of the evil god, Loki, the wicked-hearted son of Odin.

The Theft of Thor's Hammer

It was to the sweet and loving god Baldur that the earth owed its warmth and beauty, its rich fruit and its rare harvests. How the frost giants hated Baldur, and how they struggled year after year to wrest the earth from him!

They hated the warmth Baldur brought with him, for it destroyed their power. They hated the sweet flowers and the soft grass and the tiny leaves that everywhere peeped out when the winds whispered, "Baldur is coming, Baldur is coming."

But no sooner had Baldur turned away and said, "Goodbye, dear earth, for a little time, remember Baldur loves you and will come back again to you," than the frost giants would creep out from their mountain gorges, and burst forth upon the fields and forests.

The tiny bubbling brooks they would seal with their cruel chains of ice; even the great rivers could not hold their freedom against the giant power.

Like angry fiends they would seize upon the leaves and tear them from the trees. The tiny flowers hung their heads and shrivelled with fear when they approached; nor were the frost giants content until the whole earth lay brown and cold and barren beneath their hand. Then, all beauty swept away, they covered over all, their silent sheet of snow, and stood, grim sentinels, cold and hard, guarding their work of destruction and desolation.

There was deep silence when the frost giants reigned; no sound was heard save the sad moaning among the branches of the forest, as the firs and pine trees bent towards each other and whispered of the days when Baldur shone upon them.

But the frost giants never yet had conquered; never yet had Baldur failed to return to the trees and flowers and rivers and streams that he loved so well.

At his first step upon the ice, a crackling sound was heard – a sound which awoke the sleeping earth and warned the frost giants to flee to their mountains.

"Baldur has come! Baldur has come!" the birds and every living thing would cry; and a rustle and sound of music would thrill the waiting earth.

Then came always a mighty battle. The frost giants lashed the waters and rocked the trees. The winds shrieked, the sky grew cold and black. The snows fell and the driving rain beat against the earth. But Baldur, the quiet, firm, loving Baldur always conquered. How, he himself could hardly tell. He did not fight; he did not storm. He only bent his shining face over the struggling earth and waited.

Little by little, when their fury was spent, the frost giants, defiant but conquered, retreated. The great sheets of ice broke up, and the rivers rushed forth singing their mad songs of joy and freedom. The snows faded away, and one by one the little flowers peeped forth again.

All now was happiness and warmth and fragrance; the flowers bloomed; the fruits turned mellow; the sky grew warm; and the pines and fir trees breathed deep sighs of rest and contentment that once again sweet Baldur was among them.

And not only did the frost giants hate Baldur, but they hated Frey, who often robbed them of the fruits and flowers they loved to breathe their bitter breath upon and kill. Thor, too, they hated; for with his magic hammer, he now, more than ever, loved to bring forth the lightnings and the thunder, and to send down upon the earth refreshing showers of soft, warm rain.

As the frost giants scowled down from their icy castles, and saw the little flowers turn up their happy faces to drink in the sparkling drops, and heard the birds trill their happy songs, and smelled the rich fragrance of the damp firs and pines, they roared with anger and vexation.

"Let us revenge ourselves upon this insolent Thor who robs us of our rights," they bellowed to each other across the great valleys that separated their giant peaks.

"We can do nothing so long as he holds the magic hammer," growled one.

"We must steal the hammer from him," shouted another.

"Steal the hammer! Steal the hammer!" shouted all the giants until the very skies echoed with the words.

"And I will be the one to steal it," bellowed Thrym, the strongest and greatest giant of them all.

"And, moreover, I will go at once to the city of Asgard. The gods are asleep. With my great eye, I can see even now the hammer lying beside the sleeping Thor. Guard my castle. I am gone."

And putting on the guise of a great bird, Thrym spread his wings and flew across the black night to Asgard. The gods shivered in their sleep as he entered and breathed his breath upon the summer air of heaven, but knew not what had chilled them.

In the morning there was a heavy frost upon the gateways. There was a chill in the air. For Thrym, the frost giant, had crept in upon them. He had crept even to the hall in which the mighty Thor was sleeping. He had crept close beside the mighty god – and the magic hammer was gone.

"My hammer! My hammer!" thundered Thor, awaking and finding it gone.

The gods in all Asgard awoke with a start.

"What a crash of thunder! So quick, so sharp!" cried the earth-people; for they did not know it was a cry of rage from Thor.

"Loki," thundered Thor again. "Put you on wings. Go you to the home of the Frost giants and bring back my hammer. Some one of them has stolen it. Go! Go! I say."

And Loki, who had been a very obedient servant to Thor since his theft of the golden hair of Sif, put on the magic wings and fled away.

"What brings you here in the land of the Frost giants?" growled Thrym, as Loki alighted before him.

"I have come for the hammer you have stolen from Thor," answered Loki boldly, seeing at once, from the jeering look in Thrym's eye, that he was the thief.

"You will never find it," sneered Thrym. "It is well hidden; but I will send it back to you if Odin will send me Freya for my wife."

Loki begged and coaxed and threatened; but it was all of no avail. "Never," bellowed Thrym, "until you send Freya to me."

"She shall go," thundered Thor, when Loki came back to Asgard. "Whatever the price, the hammer must be brought back. Asgard is not safe without it."

But Freya was as fierce as had been Thrym himself. "I will not go," she insisted. "Never! Never! Never will I go!"

"I say you must," thundered Thor. But although Thor's thunders were terrible and his frown was deep and inky black, Freya was not to be moved either by pleading or threatening.

"Go yourself," said she. "Dress yourself as a goddess and go." Nor would she listen even to another word. Thor thundered and rumbled and rolled. It was all of no avail. Freya was a goddess and would not be driven.

"I will go," said Thor at last. "Bring me a bridal dress. Hang a necklace around my neck. Bind a bridal veil about my head. The giants are as stupid as they are large; and I will set forth in the name of Freya to meet the giant Thrym."

Thor was quickly dressed, and the bridal party set forth across the sky in the chariot of the Sun-god. How the thunder rolled! How the lightnings flashed from the angry eyes of Thor! How he grumbled and rumbled!

Jotunheim was reached. The Sun-god lowered his chariot behind the hills; and a soft, red light spread over the earth and sky as the bridal party entered the castle of the giant Thrym.

"Freya has come! Freya has come!" bellowed Thrym. "Come, come, everyone to the bridal feast! Come, come to the feast of Thrym and Freya!"

The giants in all the mountains round about answered to the call of Thrym. An hour, and the huge castle was filled with the huge guests. A great feast was held. But through it all Thor sat silent and motionless. Indeed, he dared not move; he dared not speak lest the thunder burst forth from his lips, or the lightning shoot forth from his eyes.

"Now lift the veil from Freya's face,"

bellowed Thrym, when all save the bride herself had eaten and drank their fill. "Let me see the eyes of my bride. Let us all look upon the face of my goddess bride."

"Not yet," whispered Loki coming forward; "it was the command of Thor that the veil should not be lifted, nor should you claim Freya for your own, until the hammer was placed in her hand, to be returned to the gods."

"Bring in the hammer! Bring in the hammer!" roared Thrym, full of loud, good humour.

The hammer was brought. Hardly could Thor wait to have it placed in his hand.

His thunder began to rumble. There was a dangerous light in his eyes; but Thrym and the guests saw none of this. But hardly was the hammer within his reach when forth Thor sprang, seized it in his clutched fingers, tore aside the bridal veil, and with a rumble and a roar that shook the mountains

Þor var at vio meo
hyme Jotni ɔꝛ Dregur
hier midgards Ormi
reidist Hymi ɔꝛ reider
hamarinn Miolnir, oc
vill liosta han þ Hugl
ise so sem lesa ma i XLI
Dæmi Savgu Eʃþku

of Jotunheim and razed the great stone castles to the ground, he poured out his lightnings upon the giants, one and all. Right and left he swung the mighty weapon; the giants quaked and trembled with terror; Thrym ran and hid himself behind a mountain; the air was white with lightning; the hills rang with the crashings of the thunder; the seas lashed and foamed and answered back the echoes; the walls of Jotunheim shook and trembled.

And now the chariot of the Sun-god was near at hand. Into it Thor and Loki leaped, and were borne back to the city of the gods. The hammer was restored. Again Thor held it in his mighty grasp. He held it, and Asgard once more was safe.

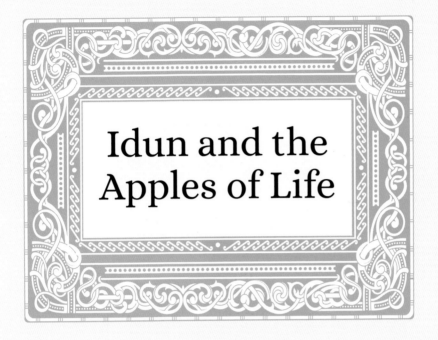

Idun and the
Apples of Life

Odin, the wise father of the gods, started off one day on a journey through Midgard, the world of men, to see how his people were getting on, and to give them help. He took with him his brother Hönir, the light-giver, and Loki, the fire-god. Loki, you know, was always ready to go wherever he could have any fun or do any mischief.

All the morning they went about among the homes of Midgard, and whenever Odin found busy, faithful workers, he was sure to leave behind some little thing which would hardly be noticed, a straw in the farmer's barn, or a kernel of grain in the furrow by the plough, or a bit of iron at the blacksmith's forge; but always happiness and plenty followed his little gift.

At noontime Loki was so hungry that he begged Odin to stop for dinner; so when they came to a shady spot by the bank of a river, the three gods chose it for their resting-place.

Odin threw himself down under a tree and began to read his little book of runes, or wise sayings, but Loki began to make a fire and get ready for the feast. Then he started off to a farmhouse near by, leaving Hönir to cook the meat which they had brought.

As Loki came near the farmhouse, he thought to himself, "I will change myself into a cat, and then I can have a better chance to spy about." So he changed himself into a black cat, and jumping upon the kitchen window-sill, he saw the farmer's wife taking some cakes out of the oven. They smelled so good and looked so tempting that Loki said to himself, "What a prize those cakes would be for our dinner!"

Just then the woman turned back to the oven to get more cakes, and Loki snatched those which she had laid on the table. The good housewife soon missed her cakes; she looked all about, and could not think what had become of them, but just as she was taking the last lot from the oven, she turned quickly around, and saw the tail of a cat whisking out of the window.

"There!" cried she, "that wicked black cat has stolen my nice cakes. I will go after him with my broom!" But by the time she reached the door all she could see was a cow walking in her garden, and when she came there to drive her away, nothing was to be seen except a big raven and six little ones flying overhead.

Then the mischievous Loki went back to the river bank, where he had left his two friends, and showed them the six cakes, boasting of the good joke he had played upon the poor woman. But Odin did not think it was a joke. He scolded Loki for stealing, and said, "It is a shame for one of the Aesir to be a thief! Go back to the farmhouse, and put these three black stones on the kitchen table."

Loki knew that the stones meant something good for the poor woman, and he did not wish to go back to the house; but he had to do as the All-father told him. As he went along he heard his friends the foxes, who put their heads out of their holes and laughed at his tricks, for the foxes thought Loki was the biggest thief of them all.

Changing himself into an owl, Loki flew in at the kitchen window, and dropped from his beak the three stones, which, when they fell upon the white table, seemed to be three black stains.

The next time the good woman came into her kitchen, she was surprised to find that the dinner was all cooked. And so

the wonderful stones that Odin had sent brought good luck; the housewife always found her food ready cooked, and all her jars and boxes filled with good things to eat, and never again was in need.

The other women all said she was the best housekeeper in the village, but one thing always troubled her, and that was the table with the three black stains. She scrubbed, and scrubbed, but could never make it white again.

And now we must go back to Loki. He was very hungry by this time, and hoped that Hönir would have the meat nicely cooked when he came back to the river bank, but when they took it out of the kettle, they found it was not cooked at all. So Odin went on reading his book of runes, not thinking about food, while Hönir and Loki watched the fire, and at the end of an hour they looked again at the meat.

"Now, it will surely be done this time!" said Loki, but again they were disappointed, for the meat in the kettle was still raw. Then they began to look about to see what magic might be at work, and at last spied a big eagle sitting on a tree near the fire. All at once the bird spoke, and said, "If you will promise to give me all the meat I can eat, it shall be cooked in a few minutes."

The three friends agreed to this, and in a short time, as the bird had promised, the meat was well done. Loki was so hungry he could hardly wait to get it out of the kettle, but suddenly the eagle pounced down upon it, and seized more than half, which made Loki so angry that he took up a stick to beat the bird, and what do you think happened? Why, the stick, as soon as it touched the bird's back, stuck fast there, and Loki found he could not let go of his end of it. Then away

flew the eagle, carrying Loki with him, over the fields and over the tree-tops, until it seemed as though his arms would be torn from his body. He begged for mercy, but the bird flew on and on. At last Loki said, "I will give you anything you ask, if you will only let me go!"

Now the eagle was really the cruel storm giant Thiassi, and he said, "I will never let you go until you promise to get for me, from Asgard, the lovely goddess Idun, and her precious apples!"

When Odin and Hönir saw Loki whisked off through the air, they knew that the eagle must be one of their giant enemies, so they hurried home to Asgard to defend their sacred city. Just as they came to Bifröst, the rainbow bridge, Loki joined them; but he took care not to tell them how the eagle came to let him go.

Odin felt sure that Loki had been doing something wrong, but knowing very well that Loki would not tell him the truth, he made up his mind not to ask any questions.

* * *

The goddess Idun, whom Loki was to tempt away out of Asgard, was the dearest of them all. She was the fair goddess of spring and of youth, and all the Aesir loved her. Her garden was the loveliest spot, with all sorts of bright, sweet flowers, birds singing by day and night, little chattering brooks under the great trees, and everything happy and fresh. The gods loved to go and sit with Idun, and rest in her beautiful garden, within the walls of Asgard.

There was another delightful thing in the garden, and that was Idun's casket. This was a magic box filled with big, golden-red apples, which she always gave her friends to taste. These

wonderful apples were not only delicious to eat, but whoever tasted them, no matter how tired or feeble he might be, would feel young and strong again. So the dwellers in Asgard ate often of this wonderful fruit, which kept them fresh and young, fit to help the people in the world of Midgard. The casket in which Idun kept her apples was always filled, for whenever she took out one, another came in its place; but no one knew where it came from, and only the goddess of youth, herself, could take the apples from the box, for if any one else tried, the fruit grew smaller and smaller, as the hand came nearer, until at last it vanished away.

A few days after Loki's bargain with the giant Thiassi, Idun was in her bright garden one morning, watering the flowers, when her husband, Bragi, came to say good-bye to her, because he must go on a journey.

Loki watched him start off, and thought, "Now, here is my chance to tempt Idun away from Asgard." After a while he went to the garden, and found the lovely goddess sitting among her flowers and birds. She looked up at Loki with such a sweet smile, as he came near, that he felt almost ashamed of his cruel plan; but he sat down on a grassy bank, and asked Idun for one of her magic apples.

After tasting it, he smacked his lips, saying, "Do you know, fair Idun, as I was coming home toward Asgard one day, I saw a tree full of apples which were really larger and more beautiful than yours; I do wish you would go with me and see them."

"Why, how can that be?" said Idun, "for Father Odin has often told me that my apples were the largest and finest he ever saw. I should so like to see those others, and I think I will go with you now, to compare them with mine."

"Come on, then!" said Loki; "and you'd better take along

your own apples, so that we can try them with the others."

Now Bragi had often told Idun that she must never wander away from home, but, thinking it would do no harm to go such a little way, just this once, she took the casket of apples in her hand and went with Loki. They had hardly passed through the garden gate, when she began to wish herself back again, but Loki, taking her by the hand, hurried along to the rainbow bridge.

They had no sooner crossed over Bifröst than Idun saw a big eagle flying toward them. Nearer and nearer he came, until at last he swooped down and seized poor Idun with his sharp talons, and flew away with her to his cold, barren home. There she stayed shut up for many long dreary months, always longing to get back to Asgard, to see Bragi and her lovely garden.

The giant Thiassi had long been planning that if he could only once get the fair goddess of youth in his power, he would eat her magic apples, and so get strength enough to conquer the Aesir; but now, after all, she would not give him even one of them, and when he put his hand into the casket, the apples grew smaller and smaller, until at last they vanished, so that he could not get even a taste.

This cruel storm giant kept poor Idun closely shut up in a little rock chamber, hoping that some day he could force her to give him what he wanted. All day long she heard the sea beating on the rocks below her gloomy cell, but she could not look out, for the only window was a narrow opening in the rock, high up above her head. She saw no one but the giant, and his serving-women, who waited upon her.

When these women first came to her, Idun was surprised to see that they were not ugly or stern-looking, and, when she looked at their fair, smiling faces, she hoped they would be friendly and pitiful to her in her trouble. She begged them to help her, and, with many tears, told them her sad story; but still they kept on smiling, and when they turned their backs, Idun saw that they were hollow. These were the Ellewomen, who had no hearts, and so could never be sorry for any one. When one is in trouble, it is very hard to be with Ellewomen.

Every day the giant came to ask Idun, in his terrible voice, if she had made up her mind to give him the apples. Idun was frightened, but she always had courage enough to say "No," for she knew it would be false and cowardly to give to a wicked giant these precious gifts which were meant for the high gods. Although it was hard to be a prisoner, and to see no one but the cold, fair Ellewomen who kept on smiling at her tears, she knew it was far better to belong to the bright Aesir, even in

prison, than to be a giant, or an Ellewoman, no matter how free or smiling they might be.

* * *

All this while the dwellers in Asgard were sad and lonely without their dear Idun. At first they went to her garden, as before, but they missed the bright goddess, and soon the garden itself grew dreary. The fresh green leaves turned brown and fell, the flowers faded, no new buds opened. No bird-songs were heard, and the saddest thing of all was that now the gods had no more of the wonderful apples to keep them fresh and strong, while two strangers, named Age and Pain, walked about the city of Asgard, and the Aesir felt themselves growing tired and feeble.

Every day they watched for Idun's return; at last, when day after day had passed, and still she did not come, a meeting of all the gods and goddesses was called to talk over what they should do, and where they should search for their lost sister.

Loki, you may be sure, took care not to show himself at the meeting; but when it was found out that Idun had last been seen walking with him, Bragi went after him, and brought him in before all the Aesir.

Then Father Odin, who sat on his high throne, looking very tired and sad, said: "Oh, Loki, what is this that you have done? You have broken your promise of brotherhood, and brought sorrow upon Asgard! Fail not to bring home again our sister, or else come not yourself within our gates!"

Loki knew well that this command must be obeyed, and besides, even he was beginning to wish for Idun again; so, borrowing the cloak of falcon feathers which belonged to the goddess Freya, he put it on and set out for Utgard and the castle

of the giant Thiassi, which was a gloomy cave in a high rock by the sea, and there he found poor Idun shut up in prison.

By good luck, the giant was away fishing when Loki arrived, so he was able to fly in, without being seen, through the narrow opening in Idun's rock cell. You would have taken him to be just a falcon bird, but Idun knew it was really Loki, and was filled with joy to see him. Without stopping to talk, Loki quickly changed her into a nut, which he held fast in his falcon claws, and flew swiftly northward, over the sea, toward Asgard. He had not gone far when he heard a rushing noise behind them, and he knew it must be the eagle. Faster and faster flew the falcon with his precious nut; but the fierce eagle flew still faster after them.

Meanwhile, for five days, the dwellers in Asgard gathered together on the city walls, gazing southward, to watch for the coming of the birds, while Loki and Idun, chased by Thiassi, the eagle, flew over the wide sea separating Utgard, the land of the giants, from Asgard. Each night the eagle was nearer his prey, and the watchers in the city were filled with fear lest he should overtake their friends.

At last they thought of a plan to help Idun: gathering a great pile of wood by the city walls, they set fire to it. When Loki reached the place he flew safely through the thick smoke and flame, for you know he was the god of fire, and dropped down into the city with his little nut held fast in his falcon claws. But when the heavy eagle came rushing on after them, he could not rise above the heat of the fire, and, smothered by the smoke, fell down and was burned to death.

There was great joy in Asgard at having the dear Idun back again; her friends gathered around her, and she invited them all into her garden, where the withered trees and flowers began to sprout and blossom; the gay birds came back, singing and building their nests, and the happy little brooks went dancing under the trees.

Idun sat with Bragi among her friends, and they all feasted upon her golden apples; she was so thankful to be free, and at home in her garden again. Once more the Aesir became young and strong, and the two dark strangers went away, for happiness and peace had come back to Asgard.

The Binding
of the Wolf

Although the Apples of Life had been brought back, and although Loki appeared for some time very penitent and willing to obey the laws of the kind Odin, the gods had little faith in him. More than that, so much had they suffered, that now they were in constant fear of him. "We never know," pleaded Freya and Sif and Idun, all of whom had good reason to fear him, "what mischief he may be planning."

And so it came about that Loki was driven forth from Asgard, as indeed he deserved to be.

Straight to the home of the giants Loki went – he always

had been a giant at heart, the evil creature! – and was much more in harmony with them in their thoughts and acts, than ever he had been with the gods whom he claimed as his people.

But now that he was cast out from Asgard, and could no longer share its beauties and its joys, he had but one wish – that was, to be revenged upon the gods, to destroy them, and to ruin their golden city.

To do this he raised two dreadful creatures. Terrible monsters! Even the gods shuddered as they looked upon them.

"Loki! Loki!" thundered Odin, looking down upon him in wrath that he should dare such vengeance.

But Loki stood defiant. There was but one thing to be done, so the gods thought; and that was to take these terrible creatures from Loki's power.

"The serpent we will cast into the sea," said Thor. "But the wolf – what shall we do with the wolf? Certainly he cannot be left to wander up and down in Midgard. The sea would not hold him. Loki must not have him in Jotunheim. What shall be done with him?"

"Kill him," said some.

"No," answered Odin. "To him Loki has given the gift of everlasting life. He will not die as long as we the gods have life. There is but one way left open to us; and that is to bring the wolf into Asgard. Here we can watch him and keep him from much, if not all the evil he would do."

And so the wolf – the Fenris-wolf he was called – was brought into the home of the gods.

He was a dreadful creature to look upon. His eyes were like balls of fire; and his fangs were white, and sharp, and cruel.

Every day he grew more terrible. Fiercer and fiercer he grew, and larger and stronger and more dreadful to look upon.

"What is to be done with him?" asked Odin one day, his face white with despair, as he looked upon the wolf, and realized what sorrow by and by he would bring among them.

"Kill him!" cried one.

"Send him to Jotunheim," cried another.

"Chain him," thundered Thor. And indeed to chain him seemed really the only thing that could be done with him.

"We will make the chains this night," said Thor. And at once the great forge was set in motion. All night long Thor worked the forge, hammering with his mighty hammer the links that should make a chain to hold the Fenris-wolf.

Morning came. The gods were filled with hope as they saw the great heap of iron. "Now we shall be safe. Now we shall be free," they said; "for no creature living can break the irons that the god of Thunder forges."

The wolf growled and showed his wicked teeth as Thor approached and threw the chain about him. He knew the gods hated him and feared him. He knew, too, that, with his wondrous strength, even the chains of Thor were not too strong for him to break.

So, snarling and showing his fangs and lashing his tail, he allowed himself to be bound. "They are afraid of me," the cruel wolf grinned. "And well they may be; there is a power in me that even they do not yet dream of."

The chains were tightly fastened, and the gods waited eagerly for the wolf to test his strength with them.

Now, the wolf knew well enough that there were no chains that could hold him. "I will amuse myself," said he to himself, "by tormenting the gods." So he glared at the chains with his fiery eyes, sniffed here and there at them, lifted one paw and then the other, bit at them with his sharp teeth, and clawed at them with his strong claws; setting up now and then a howl that echoed, like the thunders of Thor, from cloud to cloud across the skies.

The faces of the gods grew brighter and brighter. They looked at each other and hope rose high in their hearts. "We are saved!" they whispered to each other. "Hear how he howls! He knows he cannot break chains forged in the smithy of the mighty Thor."

But Odin did not smile. He knew only too well that the wolf was amusing himself; and that when the gods were least expecting it, he would spring forth and shatter the links of the mighty chain, even as a mortal might shatter a chain of straw.

"Conquered at last, you cruel Fenris-wolf!" thundered Thor, lifting his hammer in scorn, to throw at the helpless wolf.

"The Fenris-wolf is never conquered," hissed the wolf; and with one bound he leaped across the walls of Asgard, down, down across the skies to Midgard, the links of the chains scattering like sparks of fire as he flew through the air.

"See! See!" cried the people of Midgard, as they saw the fiery eyes of Fenris gleam across the sky. "See! A star has fallen! A star has fallen into the sea!" For the people of Midgard cannot understand the wonders of the heavens and the mysteries of the gods.

The gods stood, wonder-struck. Their faces were pale with fright. The brow of Thor grew black and stern. Odin looked pityingly upon them all. "Lose not your courage," said he kindly. "The Fenris-wolf shall yet be bound; and there shall yet remain to us ages upon ages of happiness and freedom from his wicked power. Go now to the dwarfs who work their forges in the great mines beneath the mountains of Midgard. They shall make for you a magic chain that even Fenris cannot break."

Hardly were the words out of Odin's mouth when Thor set forth upon the wings of his own lightning, to the home of the dwarfs, to do the bidding of Odin the All-wise.

With wonderful speed the chain was forged; and when the Sun-god lifted his head above the hills, to send forth his light

again across the fields of Midgard, the first sight that greeted his return was Thor, a great mass of golden coil within his hand, speeding up the rainbow bridge to Asgard.

It was a tiny chain – hardly larger than a thread; but in it lay a magic strength.

Entering the great golden gate, Thor saw the Fenris wolf, again creeping stealthily up and down the streets.

Thor's hand shut tight upon the handle of his hammer. It was hard to believe that a blow from the hammer would not slay the wicked creature. For an instant Thor's face grew black. Then forcing a smile, and showing to the wolf the mass of gold, he said, "Come Fenris; come with me into the hall. There the gods are to meet and test our strength upon this magic coil. Whoever breaks it, and so proves himself the strongest, is to win a prize from the great All-father Odin."

The wolf stretched back his cruel lips, and showed his sharp fangs of teeth. He did not speak; but his wicked grin said, "You do not deceive the Fenris-wolf."

Together Thor and the Fenris-wolf entered the presence of Odin and the gods and goddesses.

"I have," said Thor, "a magic coil. It is very strong. The dwarfs made it for me; and Odin has promised a great prize to the one who shall be strong enough to break its links. Come, let us try."

Then the gods – for they all understood what Thor was about to do – sprang forward, seizing the coil, pulling and twisting it in every way and in every direction, coiling it about the pillars of the hall, and hanging by it from the arches; until at last, tired out and breathless, they sank exhausted upon the golden floors.

"Fenris," called Thor. "Now is your time to prove to us

what you have so often said – that you are stronger than we. Try if you can break this golden thread which, small as it is, has proved too strong for the strength of the gods."

The wolf growled. He did not care to risk even his strength in a magic coil. He growled and slunk away.

"What! Fenris, are you a coward? After all your boasted strength, why is it that you shrink from a contest in which the gods have willingly taken part? Do you mean to say that, because the gods have been defeated, you fear that you, too, may be defeated?"

The wolf halted. He looked back at the gods and growled a long, low growl. The words of Thor had stung his pride.

Thor laughed. "O Fenris, Fenris! this is your boasted

strength! your boasted courage! To slink away in a contest with the gods – the gods at whose strength you have always sneered and scoffed."

"Fenris is a coward!" cried all the gods; and the heavens echoed with their laughter.

This was more than the wolf could bear. Back he sprang into the hall.

"I hear your sneers," he snarled. "I hear you call me coward. Give me the cord; bind me with it round and round; fasten me to the strongest pillar of this great hall. If the coil is an honest coil, Fenris can break it. There is no chain he cannot break. But if you are blinding me – if you have here a cord woven with magic such as no power can break – how am I to know? I put this test to you. Some one of you shall place your hand between my jaws. As long as that hand is there, you may coil

and coil the thread about me. Then, if I find the cord a magic cord, Fenris shall set his teeth upon the hand and crush it."

The gods stared at one another. Surely, Thor must not lose his hand. Thor needed his hand with which to wield the magic hammer.

Then Tyre, the brave god Tyre, the god of courage and bravery and unselfishness stepped forth.

"Here is my hand, O Fenris-wolf. It shall be yours to destroy if you can not loose yourself when bound in the golden coil."

Again the Fenris-wolf showed his shining teeth. He seized the hand between his heavy jaws; Thor bound the cord about him. "Now free yourself," he thundered. "Free yourself, and prove to the gods the mighty power of the Fenris-wolf."

The wolf, his eyes blazing with wrath, and with fear as well, struggled with the coil. But alas for the wolf! And joy for the gods! The harder he struggled, the fiercer he battled, the tighter drew the cord. With a howl of rage that shook the city and echoed even to the base of the great Mount Ida, he seized upon the hand of Tyre and tore it from his wrist. With another angry howl he sprang towards Thor; but with a quick turn Thor seized one end of the coil, fastened it to a great rock, and before the wolf could set his fangs he hurled him, rock and all, over the walls of the city, down down into the mighty sea.

"And there, chained to his rocky island, he shall abide forever," cried the gods; "and now peace once more shall rest upon our city."

But Odin sighed, and to himself he said, "O happy children, there shall yet come a day when darkness shall fall upon us; the Fenris-wolf shall again be loosed; and even the gods shall be no more."

Freya's Necklace

"Yes, I really must have some flowers to wear to the feast to-night," said Freya to her husband, Odur.

Freya was the goddess of love and beauty; she was the most beautiful of all the Aesir, and every one loved to look at her charming face, and to hear her sweet voice.

"I think you look quite beautiful enough as you are, without flowers," Odur replied, but Freya was not satisfied; she thought she would go and find her brother Frey, the god of summer, for he would give her a garland of flowers. So she wandered forth from Asgard on her way to Frey's bright home in Alfheim, where he lived among his happy, busy little elves. As Freya walked along she was thinking of the feast to be given that night in Asgard, and knowing that all the gods and goddesses would be there, she wished to look her very best.

On and on she wandered, not thinking how far she was getting away from home. Finally the light began to grow fainter and fainter, and Freya found herself in a strange place. The sunlight had faded away, but there was still a little light that came from lanterns carried by funny little dwarfs, who were busily working. Some were digging gold and gems, others were cleaning off the dirt from the precious stones, and polishing them to make them bright, while four little fellows were seated in one corner, putting the sparkling stones together into a wonderful necklace.

"What can that beautiful thing be?" thought Freya. "If only I had that, it would surely make me look more beautiful than any one else at the feast to-night!" And the more she thought about it, the more she longed to get it. "Oh, I really must have it!" she said to herself, and with these words she stepped nearer to the four little men. "For what price will you sell me your necklace?" she asked.

The dwarfs looked up from their work, and when they saw Freya's lovely face and heard her sweet voice, said, "Oh, if you will only look kindly upon us, and be our friend, you may have the necklace!"

Then a mocking laugh echoed again and again through the dark cavern, seeming to say, "How foolish you are to

wish for these bright diamonds; they will not make you happy!" But Freya snatched the necklace and ran out of the cavern. It did not please her to hear the teasing laugh of the dwarfs, and she wanted to get away from them as soon as possible.

At last she was once more out in the open air; she tried to be free and happy again, but a strange feeling of dread came over her, as if something were going to happen. Soon she came to a still pool of water, and, putting on the necklace, she bent over to look at her picture in the clear water. How beautiful the diamonds were! and how they sparkled in the sunshine! She must hasten home to show them to Odur.

The fair goddess soon reached Asgard, and hurried to the palace to find her husband. But Odur was not there. Over and over again she searched through all the rooms in vain; he had gone, and although Freya had her beautiful necklace, she cared little for it without her dear husband.

Soon it was time to go to the feast, but Freya would not go without Odur. She sat down and wept bitter tears; she felt no

joy now for having the necklace, and no sorrow because she could not feast with the Aesir.

If only Odur would come back, all would be well again. "I will go to the end of the world to find him!" said Freya, and she began to make ready for her journey. Her chariot, drawn by two cats, was soon ready; but before she could start, she must first ask Father Odin to allow her to go.

"All-father, I beg you give me leave to go to look for my Odur in every corner of the world!"

The wise father replied, "Go, fair Freya, and may you find whom you seek."

Then she started forth. First to the Midgard world the goddess of beauty went, but no one in all the world had seen or heard of Odur. Down under the earth, to Niflheim, and even to Utgard, the land of giants, she wandered, but still no one had seen or even heard of her husband. Poor Freya wept many tears, and wherever the teardrops fell, and sank into the ground, they turned into glistening gold.

At last the sad goddess returned to her own palace alone. She still wore the wonderful necklace, which was called Brisingamen.

One night, when the hour was late, all the Aesir were asleep, except the ever watchful Heimdall, who heard soft footsteps, like those of a cat, near Freya's palace. He listened, and thought, "That is surely some one bent on mischief; I must follow him."

When Heimdall reached the palace, he found it was Loki, changed into another form, creeping softly about. Heimdall quietly watched him, and saw him glide in to Freya's bedside, where the fair goddess lay asleep, wearing her beautiful necklace. Loki had come to steal the necklace, but when he saw that she was lying on the clasp of the chain, so that he could not undo it without waking her, he changed himself into a gnat, and, crawling along on the pillow, stung her just enough to make her turn over, but not enough to wake her. Then he unclasped the chain and ran off with it as fast as he could.

But Heimdall was not going to let the thief get away. As soon as Loki found that he was followed, he took his other form, a little flame of fire; Heimdall then took *his* other shape, and became a shower of rain, to put out the fire; but Loki, quick and watchful, changed himself into a bear, to catch the rain.

Then Heimdall too became a bear, and a fierce fight began. At last the rain-god conquered, and forced wicked Loki to give back the necklace to Freya.

The whole land seemed to feel sorry for poor, lonely Freya; the leaves fell from the trees, the bright flowers faded, and the singing birds flew away.

Once more the fair goddess went forth from Asgard to seek Odur. Away, away to the far-off sunny south she wandered, and there, where the myrtle trees and the oranges grow, at last she found her long-lost husband.

Then hand in hand the two turned northward again, to their home, and so happy were they together, that they spread joy and happiness around them as they passed along. Everywhere the ice and snow thawed before them, green grass and sweet flowers sprang up behind their footsteps, the birds sang their sweetest songs, the warm summer came back to the north lands, and every one was glad and joyful, for lovely, smiling Freya was at home again.

> "White were the moorlands
> And frozen, before her;
> Green were the moorlands
> And blooming, behind her.
> Out of her gold locks
> Shaking the spring flowers,
> Out of her garments
> Shaking the south wind,
> Around in the birches
> Awaking the throstles,
> Beautiful Freya came."
> — Kingsley

The Adventures of Thor

PART I

Greatest among the giants of Jotunheim, was Hrungner. Even the gods stood in fear of him; for when Thor's deep thunder rolled out across the skies, and the winds rose and the clouds grew black, it was Hrungner who, bold and defiant, shouted back with roars of scornful laughter – roars that rivalled in their thunder those of the great and mighty Thor.

"This giant," said the gods, standing in council together, "this giant must be overcome. Too long have we suffered him to defy our power; too long have we borne his insolence; too long have his threats passed unnoticed by Odin the All-father and by Thor the god of Thunder."

"I will go forth," said Odin, "upon my winged horse, my fleet-footed Sleipner, to meet this giant who dares defy the gods of Asgard."

Accordingly across the skies, over the sea to Jotunheim, rode Odin.

"It is a fine steed you ride, good stranger," bellowed Hrungner as Odin drew near; "almost as fine a steed as my own Goldfax, who can fly through the air and swim through the seas with the same ease that another steed might travel upon the plains of Midgard."

"But his speed cannot equal that of Sleipner," answered Odin quietly, his deep eyes burning with the light no giant could quite comprehend, and beneath which even Hrungner quailed at heart.

"Sleipner! Odin!" thundered Hrungner. "Are you Odin? And is this your Sleipner – the winged steed of which the gods of Asgard boast? Away with him! And I upon my Goldfax will prove to you that in Jotunheim lives one giant who dares challenge even Odin and his mighty war-horse to contest. Away! Away Odin! Away Sleipner! Away Hrungner! Away Goldfax!"

And with a shout that echoed even to the halls of Asgard, the great giant mounted his steed and soon brought him, neck to neck with Odin and his immortal Sleipner.

On, on, across the skies they flew. Before their mighty force, the clouds scattered hither and thither, striking against each other with a crashing sound that to the earth-people was like the voice of Thor.

From the eyes of the steeds the lightnings flashed; and from their reeking sides the foam fell in showers upon the earth below. The people, terror-stricken, ran to their caves and prayed the gods to protect them from the fury of the blast.

"It is like no storm we ever knew," they whispered, one to the other. "The thunder! the lightnings! the scurrying clouds! and with it all, the roaring winds and the falling of great white flakes, now like hail, now like snow! Has Odin forgotten his children? Have the Frost giants fallen upon Asgard?" But now

the storm was over. Odin and Hrungner both had reached the walls of Asgard. Through the great rolling gateway both had burst together; for the steed of the bold Hrungner had indeed proved himself equal to the snow-white Sleipner, whose magic powers no one but Odin fully knew.

Hrungner, elated with his success, and never once dreaming that, had Odin so willed it, he, with his brave steed Goldfax, might have been left far behind in the race, strode into the halls of Asgard and called loudly for food and drink and rest.

All these were granted him, and the giant threw himself down upon a golden couch and stared insolently upon the gods. All were there save Thor. "And where," bellowed Hrungner, "is the great god Thor, the mighty thunderer who dares defy the Frost giants; and whose strength is boasted greater than that of Hrungner, the chief of the mighty Frost giants?

"Bring him into my presence," roared the giant. "Let me prove to you that one giant at least dares defy even the greatest and most warlike of you all."

Away upon the sea, Thor heard this boast. "Who challenges me and defies my power?" he thundered; and with the swiftness of the wind, hastening upward toward the shining city, he burst in upon the giant stretched out upon the golden couch.

"I challenge you!" bellowed the giant, springing from his couch and facing the god of thunder.

Thor raised his hammer. The lightnings flashed from his eye. "Halt!" roared the giant. "Little credit will it be to the god of Thunder to fall in battle upon a Frost giant unarmed and unprotected. You are a coward! Fight me as becomes a great god on equal grounds and under fair conditions. Come to me in the land of Jotunheim, and there will I challenge you to battle. Then will your victory, if you win, lend lustre to your greatness; and the fear of you throughout the land of the Frost giants be greater than ever before."

"As you say," answered Thor with a sneer. "Go now, and make ready for the holmgang in which the insolent, boastful Hrungner shall learn the power of the gods whom, in his ignorance, he dares defy."

Then Hrungner departed from the city of Asgard, and assembled the giants together to prepare for the coming battle. "Let us make a giant of clay," and at once every giant in Jotunheim fell to work. Whole mountains were levelled to the earth, and the great masses of stone and earth heaped high; until, on the third day, there stood a giant nine miles high and three miles broad, ready to defy the power of the Thunder-god when he should come. But alas for the heart of this warrior of clay! None could be found, either in Midgard or in Jotunheim, of size proportionate to the body of the mighty creation; and so, in despair, the heart of a sheep was chosen, and around it the clay warrior was built.

At the first sound of rolling thunder – by which the coming of Thor was announced afar off – alas! this heart, fluttering and trembling, so shook the mighty form that its spear fell from its hand, its knees shook, and Hrungner was left to fight his battle alone with the angry son of Odin.

Onward, nearer and nearer, came Thor the Terrible. The lightnings flashed and the earth rumbled. Seizing a great mountain of flint in his hands, Hrungner waited. His eyes burned and his face was set.

Suddenly, forth from the ground beneath his feet, the god of Thunder burst. Hrungner sprang forward. With a mighty force he hurled the mountain of flint. Thor, with a roar, flung his mighty hammer. The two crashed together in midair. The flint broke, and one half of it was driven into the heavy skull of Thor. The hammer, cleaving the flint, sped onward, and Hrungner fell dead beneath its never-failing blow; but in falling his great body lay across the neck of Thor, who, stunned by the blow from the flint, had fallen, his hammer still clenched firmly in his powerful hand.

For a moment, there was a hush. The very sun stood still. Not a sound was heard through Jotunheim. The thunder of battle had died away; all the earth was still.

Then came Magne, a son of Thor. "Why this sudden quiet?" he called. "Why has my father's voice been stilled? Certainly the great god Thor has not fallen in battle!"

"In the name of Odin," he thundered, as he saw the Frost giant's body lying across his father's massive frame, "in the name of Odin and of Thor, what does this mean?" And, seizing the giant by a foot, he hurled him out over the seas. For miles and miles the giant's body cut the air, and then, falling, sank and was buried beneath the waves.

Thor staggered to his feet again, and with a roar that made the leaves of Yggdrasil tremble and shook even the halls of Valhalla, set forth across the seas, never once looking back towards the land of Jotunheim, whose people for the time, at least, were again subdued by the power of Thor, the god of Thunder – by Thor, the son of Odin the All-wise.

There was peace in all the lands; stilled were the Frost giants, and in Midgard all was happiness.

"Come with me, that I may see that you do no mischief," said Thor to Loki, as he sprang into his golden chariot, drawn by his snow-white goats.

All day the chariot wheeled on and on across the skies. Night fell, and the gods, entering a peasant's cottage, asked for shelter. "Our supper we have with us," Thor said. And taking the goats from the chariot, he killed them and placed them before the fire.

Never had the peasants taken part in such a feast. "It is a feast for the gods," they said; "but pray, how will you finish your journey without your goats?"

"We will attend to that," said Thor. "Eat what you will, and all you can. I only ask that, when the feast is finished, you promise to place all the bones together there before the door upon the goat skins. See to it that no bone is forgotten; and that not one – even the smallest – be lost or broken."

The peasants promised; the meat was eaten, and in due time the household went to bed and to sleep.

Morning came; and with the first flush of light Thor arose, and, with his magic hammer, sat down beside the heap of bones, that lay upon the goat skins before the door.

"Kling! Kling! Kling!" sounded the hammer, striking in turn each little bone; then the two goats leaped forth, as white

and plump and round as ever, and as ready to spin across the waters with the golden chariot of their master.

But alas, one goat was lame. He held up one tiny foot and moaned. "Some one of you," roared Thor, "has broken a bone. Did I not command that you be careful, and see that every bone should be placed, uninjured, upon the goat skins?"

The peasants shook with fear. They knew now who this strange guest might be. "It is Thor!" they whispered to each other. "And that is the mighty hammer whose aim never fails, and whose force is death to all upon whom it falls!"

"O thou great god Thor," cried the peasants, "spare us! Indeed had we known, not one bone would we have taken in our unhappy fingers; and all night long would we have watched beside the goat skins that no harm should come to them. Spare us, O spare us, great Thor! Take all we have – our house, our cattle, our children, everything – only spare our lives to us!"

Thor seized his hammer in his hand. His great knuckles grew white, so strong was his giant hold upon the handle. The peasants sank upon their knees. Their faces dropped and their eyes closed. Shaking with terror, they awaited the falling of the hammer.

"Up, up, ye peasants," thundered Thor. "This offence I forgive. Your lives too, shall be spared you; but I will carry away with me these children of yours, Thjalfe and Roskva; and they shall serve me in my journeys across the lands and over the seas."

"The goats I leave with you; and I charge you, by your lives see that no harm comes to them in any way. Come Thjalfe, come Roskva, place yourselves before the chariot, and bear me quickly across the seas."

All day long the chariot wheeled on and on, the children never tiring, until, at nightfall, they found themselves upon the shores of the country of the Frost giants.

Plunging into a deep forest, they hurried through and came out into a great plain beyond. Here they found a house, the very doors of which were as high as the mountains and as broad as the broadest river.

"We will rest here," said Thor, and, spreading the great skins which they found near the doorway, they made for themselves beds, and soon were fast asleep.

At midnight they were awakened by a terrible roar. The whole house shook with its vibrations. Thor, seizing his hammer in his strong right hand, strode to the door. The whole earth trembled, but in the darkness even Thor could not see beyond the doorway.

Hour after hour he stood there, listening. Slowly, at last, the dawn began to come; the sun rose, and there, just at the edge of the forest, Thor saw the outstretched body of a giant, whose head was in itself a small mountain, and whose feet stretched away into the valley below.

"And it is you, then, that have rocked the very earth with your giant snores, and have taken from me my night of rest," thought Thor, when he saw the giant form stretched out before him.

With one angry stride Thor reached the side of the sleeping giant. Raising his hammer a full mile into the air, he smote the giant full upon the skull, with a crash that sounded like the fall of a mighty oak.

"What is that?" asked the giant, opening his sleepy eyes. "Indeed, Thor, are you here? Something awoke me. I think an acorn must have dropped upon my head," said the giant, gathering himself to rise.

"Go to sleep again," growled Thor; "it isn't morning yet. I am going to sleep myself."

A few minutes and the snores of the giant rang through the air again.

"Now we will see," thought Thor. Again he crept to the giant's side. Lifting his hammer, this time two miles in the air,

he brought it down upon the giant's skull with a crash that sounded like the breaking of the ice and the roaring of the torrent in a mighty river.

"What is that?" muttered the giant, only half awake. "A leaf must have fallen upon my forehead. I will take myself out into the plain where I can sleep in peace."

"Go to sleep," answered Thor; "it is nearly morning, and will be time to wake up for the day before you reach the plain."

Again the giant fell asleep; and again the snoring rang out upon the air. "He shall not escape me this time," whispered Thor, creeping again to the giant's side. Raising his hammer,

this time three miles in the air, he crashed it down upon the forehead of the giant with such force and fury that the very heavens reverberated; and the earth-people, springing frightened from their deep sleep, called to each other, "The dwarfs are at their forges! Did you not feel the earth shake and the mountains tremble?"

"Well, well," droned the sleepy giant; "the moss from the trees falls upon my face and wakes me. It is nearly sunrise, and I may as well arise and go on to Utgard. And you, Thor – I am told you, too, are journeying towards the land of Utgard. But I must hurry on. I will meet you there; but let me give you warning that we are a race of giants of no mean size. And great though you are, it would be as well for you that you boast not of your power among us. Even your mighty hammer might fail to do its work among giants of such strength and stature as those of Skrymer's race."

There was a sneer on Skrymer's face as he said this; but before Thor could raise his hammer to punish him for his insolence, he had crossed the great plain, and was already miles away. Thor sat down beside the forest. He was mortified, and vexed, and puzzled. What did it mean? Had his hammer lost its magic power? Was the giant Skrymer immortal? He could not tell. There was a heavy cloud upon his face as he set forth again upon his journey. The little servants shook with fear; even Loki kept silent, and said not one word the live-long day.

The Adventures
of Thor
PART II

Travelling on and on, through many days and many nights, Thor and his companions came to a great castle. Its pinnacles reached far up among the clouds, and its great gateways were broad even like the horizon itself.

In between the bars crept Thor and Loki and the children Thjalfe and Roskva.

"Let us enter the castle," said Thor grimly. "It must be the palace of the king – the Utgard-Loki – whose threats have defied even the All-wisdom and the All-power of the mighty Odin."

At these words the walls of the castle trembled. The pillars of frost and the great arches of ice glittered and glistened. Thjalfe and Roskva grew white with fear. "We hear your voice," thundered Thor; "but we have no fear of you even though you shake the castle walls until they fall. And behold, we dare come into your very presence, thou terrible king of Utgard!"

The great king showed his glittering teeth. His brow grew black with rage.

"This is Thor, the god of Thunder," he sneered: "and so small are you that you can creep through the bars of our gateway, pass unnoticed by our sentinels, even into the very presence of the king!"

Then Utgard-Loki – for this was the king's name – threw back his head and laughed until the whole earth shook; trees were uprooted, and avalanches of ice and snow, pouring down into valleys, buried hundreds of the little people of Midgard.

Thor clenched his hammer. He dared not thunder; even his lightnings were as nothing in this great palace hall and before the terrible voice of the Utgard-king.

"But perhaps you are greater than you look," continued the king, roaring again at his own wit. "Tell me what great feats you can accomplish; for no one is allowed entrance to this castle who cannot perform great deeds."

"I can perform great deeds – many of them," boasted Loki, nowise abashed, even in the presence of the terrible king. "I

can eat faster than any creature in Midgard, in Utgard, or even in Asgard, the home of the gods."

Again the king roared; and, placing before him a great wooden trough heaped high with food, he commanded his servant Loge to challenge Loki to the contest.

But alas for Loki, although the food disappeared before him like fields of grain beneath the scythe of steel, yet before the task was half begun, Loge had swallowed food, and trough, and all!

The king roared louder still; and Loki, never before beaten by giant power, shrank away, angry and threatening.

"But I," said Thjalfe, "can run. I can outrun any creature that lives on land or sea."

Then Thjalfe was placed beside a tiny little pigmy – Huge he was called; but hardly had they run a pace before Huge had shot so far ahead that Thjalfe, crestfallen, went and hid himself behind the great ice pillar that stood outside the castle gate.

And now Thor rose to his feet and drew himself up to his greatest height; but even that seemed as nothing compared with the enormous stature of the Utgard-king. He clenched the hammer tightly and thundered as never he had thundered before. The tiny fringe of icicles trembled. Then Utgard-Loki laughed; and with his thunder the whole castle rocked and reeled.

"And will Thor contest with the power of Utgard?" asked the king. "I will," roared Thor, and there was a fire in his eye that even Utgard shrank before.

But Utgard only roared in turn and brought to Thor a great horn, filled to its brim with sparkling water.

"Drink," said he; "and if one half the power is yours that Odin claims, you will empty the horn at a single draught."

Thor seized the horn. One long, deep draught, such as no mortal, no giant, nor even another god could have drawn – and the horn was hardly one drop less full.

The king roared till the icicles and the fringes of frost, swaying and rocking beneath the thunder, fell with a crash upon the palace floor.

"Can the great god Thor boast no greater power than that? Once more, thou greatest of all the sons of Odin – once more lift the horn in thy mighty hands and show us the greatness of the gods of Asgard."

Thor, stung by the sneer of the Utgard-king, raised the horn again to his lips; and calling upon the name of Odin and all the gods of the shining city, drank again. Higher and higher he raised the horn, deeper and deeper drew he the draught. But alas, again, when the horn was lowered, the waters were no lower than before.

"You seem not so great as we the frost giants have believed," said the king with a cold sneer.

Thor's anger rose. His blood boiled with rage and fury. With a burst of thunder and a flash of lightning that shattered the pillars of the great hall, he seized the horn again. Three long hours passed. Utgard-Loki trembled with fear and dread; for never for one second had the angry god taken the horn from his lips. "The ruin of the Utgard kingdom is come," he groaned. "There is no hope for victory over such a god. The horn – even the magic horn – will fail before the might of this fierce and awful Thor, the god of Thunder."

Then Thor lifted the horn from his lips. Defiance flashed from his eye. The king of the Frost giants trembled. Both looked into the horn. Alas for Thor! Even now hardly could it be counted one quarter emptied. Darkness gathered over the

strong god's face. Courage sprang into the eyes of the king. "Let not your valour fail you," said the king, taking the horn from the hand of Thor. "You are great – you have proved it, in that you have, even in so small a degree as this, emptied the horn from which none but a god could have quaffed one drop. It is only that your greatness is less than you have boasted, and less than we have believed it to be."

"I will not stand defeated," thundered Thor. "Bring before me another challenge. I will not go forth until the giants of Utgard have indeed known and felt the power of Thor, the god whose lightnings rend the skies, and whose thunders rock the very mountains of the earth."

"Once more, then, shall you contend for power," said the Utgard-king. "And this time with Elle, the toothless giant of endless years, before whose power bend all the strongest sons of Midgard, and before whom, in some far off day, even the gods of Asgard shall bow as powerless as the children of Midgard."

Thor sprang upon the giant Elle. Like a demon of the under world he fought, and for a time even this All-conquering giant swayed before the wild madness of his bursts of thunder, and his crashing, hissing bolts of fire. But alas for Thor! Even his godlike strength was doomed to fail him. He trembled; his sight vanished; a strange chill settled over him, and he sank, conquered, before the power of the giant Elle.

And now the night had fallen upon the land. The light had faded from the mountain tops; and the chill of night was in the frosty air. Exhausted, the great god wrapped himself about and sank into heavy sleep. And his dreams were of great battles, of terrible foes, and of the last great day which, sometime in the ages to come, should fall upon the city of the gods, and in which even the power of Odin should fail, and the light go out

from all the earth. All night long these dreams haunted the great heart of Thor; and in the morning the people in Midgard said, "It was a strange night. Through all the hours of darkness, the thunders rolled in the distance, and the pale lightnings flashed among the mountain peaks beyond the seas."

In the morning, even with the first rays of light, Thor, with Loki and Thjalfe and Roskva, set forth upon their journey homeward. There was a terrible blackness upon the face of Thor, and the thunders rumbled deeply. Never before had Thor

known the bitterness of defeat, and he returned to Asgard and to Odin sick at heart.

"Lose not thy courage, Thor," said the All-wise. "Know that thou art not even now defeated in any test of true strength. Utgard-Loki has triumphed to be sure; but even he trembles now, and has closed the doors of his castle, and has set thousands upon thousands of sentinels to watch against thy return.

"The horn from which thou didst drink reached far down into the depths of the sea; and the people of Midgard even now throng the shores and wonder what power in heaven or in earth can so have shrunken the great waters of the sea.

"Loge, with whom Loki contended, was none less than Wild Fire; and Huge was Thought itself. Even the gods, even Odin himself, with these would but contend in vain. And Elle – it is indeed as Utgard-Loki said – no power in heaven itself can equal hers. She is the all-powerful, the never-failing, the ever-present Old Age. All the people of the earth, all the gods of Asgard – aye, even the earth and Asgard must one day fall before her mighty will. That you contended even as you did, has driven terror deep into the hearts of the cruel Frost giants; nor do they doubt that you are the terrible god of Thunder, the greatest of all the sons of Odin."

With these words of Odin, Thor's courage rose. "Bring me my hammer," he called to Sif, "and again will I go forth into the realms of the Frost giants."

The great Odin smiled. "Fear not, my son. Remember there can be no defeat to Thor, the son of Odin, whose mighty hand holds firm the terrible hammer forged by the dwarfs of the under world."

Then Thor sprang into his chariot. "Away, away," he thundered, "to the home of Hymer – the hateful, boastful

Hymer! Away to the land of the Frost giants! Once, and for all, Thor will prove to them the power and the terror of the gods of Asgard."

The wheels of the chariot rumbled and rolled. From their spokes the lightnings flashed. With the speed of Thought itself, it hissed and whistled through the air. The clouds, scattering, raised a mighty wind.

In Midgard the leaves ran like fire before the gale; the trees rocked; and ever and anon the moaning wind rose and fell like the voice of a mighty tempest.

"It is the Valkyries!" the people of Midgard said. "Always does the wind rise; always do the clouds hurry across the skies when the Valkyries set forth to battle. Somewhere there is war in our fair earth; somewhere heroes are falling on the bloody battlefield."

For, in all this time, there had come to be many people in Midgard. The children of Ask and Embla had become men and women, had grown old, and their children, too, had become men and women.

And there were wars in the land. Warriors in the east fought those in the west; those in the north fought those in the south.

But the warriors were brave men; and over every battle Odin watched, grinding the spears, now shielding and protecting, now forcing the warriors into the very heat of the battle. And when the battle was over, and all was quiet, when the great sun had sunk behind the hills of Jotunheim, and the soft moon shone down upon the battlefield, then Odin would call to the Valkyries, and bid them go down into Midgard and bring with them to Valhalla all who had fallen bravely fighting. For this was the hero's reward. With this hope he entered battle; with this hope he fought; with this hope he turned his dying eyes

towards Mount Ida and thanked the All-father that now he, too, might enter into the joys of Asgard and know the glory of immortal life in the golden halls of Valhalla.

And now the winds had died away; the clouds were at rest; there was peace over Midgard. For the chariot had reached the home of the Frost giants, and Thor had entered the great rock-bound castle of the giant Hymer.

"Let us go out upon the sea to fish," said Thor to the dread giant, with whom he longed to measure power.

Seizing the oars, Thor himself rowed the great boat out into the sea. "Give me the oars," bellowed Hymer; "you have already rowed a long way and must be wearied."

"I wearied!" thundered Thor. "Indeed I have not rowed one half the distance. I shall row even into the realm of the Midgard Serpent, whose length lies coiled round about Midgard, and whose home is deep down beneath the raging waters. There only shall we find fish worthy of the bait of a god."

Hymer trembled. He feared the Midgard Serpent, whose great coils so lashed the waters of the ocean that they rose, white with foam, even to the very mountain tops. "The fishing just here has never failed. There is no need to row farther into the ocean," said Hymer, hoping to dissuade the god from rowing farther from the shores of Jotunheim. "But I must fish in mid-ocean, and in the deepest of the waters," was Thor's reply.

For hours and hours they rowed. The mountain tops grew dimmer and dimmer in the blue distance; no land could be seen; the waters sparkled and shone on every side as far as the eye could reach.

"We will make this our fishing place," said Thor, at last, throwing down his oars and preparing the great cable that

should serve him for a line. This he gave into the hands of the trembling giant, and prepared for himself another. The hours passed, but no fish had been drawn into the boat.

"Had you listened to me," thundered Hymer, "our boat might long before this have been filled with the fish I have never failed to catch in waters nearer the shores of the land of the Frost giants."

"Do you think a god would be content with less than the greatest fish in all the sea?" thundered Thor. "Do you not know I shall bring to this boat's edge the terrible Midgard Serpent itself?"

And even as he spoke he gathered in his line, and dashed upon the boat floor a whale of such enormous size that even the giant looked with amazement upon so terrible a display of the fisherman's strength and power. Surely this must be Thor himself!

"The whale is yours," muttered Thor, unfastening his line and throwing it overboard again. "I have no care for fish as small as this."

Suddenly there was a rush of waters. It was as if a terrible tempest had burst upon the sea. The waters seethed and foamed. The great waves rose mountain high. The boat rocked and reeled, and the green waters, pouring over its sides, filled it so that the great whale floated out upon the sea.

"It is the Midgard Serpent!" roared Thor; and his mighty voice, rising even above the rush of the great sea, mingled with the thunder of the breaking waves and echoed out to the shores of the farthest lands.

Thor sprang from the boat and planted himself firmly upon the great rocks beneath the sea. The giant, dumb with terror, clung to the sides of the rocking boat. On, on came the serpent,

nearer and nearer, the roaring waves and the heaping foam bursting closer and closer upon the mountain-like boat that tossed now like seaweed upon the angry waters.

One burst like thunder, and the terrible serpent's head rose above the foam and glistened in the light. Thor sprang forward; and, with his mighty arm, threw the cable about the slimy neck of the Midgard Serpent and dragged him to the boat's edge. The giant sprang to his feet.

"Give me my hammer!" thundered the god.

"I will not!" thundered the giant; and with one quick bound he sprang forward, raised his shining sword, and with a sweep miles high, cut the great cable which held the writhing serpent.

Another roar, and the great serpent arched his back even to

the blue dome of the sky above. Then, with a hiss that sounded through Midgard and even up to the shining city of the fair Mount Ida, he shot down beneath the waters, and over him closed the angry waves.

The foam dashed mountains high; the caves howled and boomed; the skies echoed crash on crash; and the whole earth trembled with the upheaval of the troubled waters. A rushing back, a heaping up, a breaking of great waves – and never again, by man or giant or god, was the loathsome serpent seen above the waters, until on that last sad, fateful day when the light had gone out from the sun, and the dread chill of Ragnarök had fallen even upon Valhalla and the beautiful shining city of Asgard.

Baldur and the Mistletoe Spear

Ages upon ages had rolled away. And now the day of sorrow, which always Odin had known must come, drew near.

Already the god of song had gone with his beautiful wife Idun down into the dark valley of death; and there was a new strange rustle among the leaves of Yggdrasil, like the rustling of leaves that were dead.

Odin's face grew sad; and, try as he would, he could not join with the happy gods about him in their joys and festal games.

"Odin," said Frigg one day, "tell me what grieves thee; what weighs thee down and puts such sadness into thine eyes and heart."

"Baldur himself shall tell you all," answered Odin sadly.

Then Baldur seated himself in the midst of the gods and said: "Always, since Odin drank at the Well of Wisdom, and learned the secrets of the past and of the future, has he known that a time would come when the light must go out from

Baldur's eyes; and he, although a god, must go down into the dark valley. Now that time draws near. Already have Brage and Idun gone from us; and with them have gone song and youth. Soon will Baldur go, and with him must go the light and warmth he has always been so glad to bring to Asgard and to Midgard both."

"O Baldur! Baldur! Baldur! My child! my child! my child!" cried Frigg. "This cannot be! this shall not be! I will go down from Asgard. I will go up and down the earth, and every rock and tree and plant shall pledge themselves to do no harm to thee."

"Dear mother Frigg," sighed Baldur, "you cannot change what is foretold. From the beginning of time this was decreed, that one day the light should go out from heaven and the twilight of the gods should fall."

There was a long silence in the hall of Asgard. No god had courage to speak. Their hearts were heavy, and they had no wish to speak.

The sun sank behind the western hills. Its rich sunset glow spread over the golden city and over the beautiful earth below. Then darkness followed slowly, slowly creeping, creeping on, up the mountain side, across the summit, until even the shining city stood dark and shadowy beneath the gathering twilight.

"Like this, some day, the twilight will fall upon our city," said Odin; "and it will never, never rise again."

The mother heart of Frigg would not accept even Odin's word. And when the sun's first rays shot up above the far-off hills, Frigg stole forth from Asgard down the rainbow bridge to Midgard.

To every lake, and river, and sea, she hurried, and said: "Promise me, O waters, that Baldur's light shall never go out because of you."

"We promise," the waters answered. And Frigg hurried on to the metals. "Promise me, O metals, that Baldur's light shall never go out because of you."

"We promise," answered the metals. And Frigg hurried on to the minerals. "Promise me, O minerals," she said, "that Baldur's light shall never go out because of you."

"We promise," answered the minerals. And Frigg hurried on to the fire, the earth, the stones, the trees, the shrubs, the grasses, the birds, the beasts, the reptiles; and even to the abode of pale disease she went. Of each she asked the same earnest, anxious question; and from each she received the same kind, honest answer.

As the sun sank behind the high peaks of the Frost giants' homes, Frigg, radiant and happy, her eyes bright and her heart alive with hope, sped up the rainbow bridge. Triumphant, she hurried into the great hall to Odin and Baldur.

"Be happy again, O Odin! Be happy again, O Baldur! There is no danger, no sorrow to come to us from anything in the

earth or under the earth. For every tree has promised me; and every rock and every metal; every animal and every bird. Even the waters and the fire have promised that never harm through them shall come to Baldur."

But, alas, for poor Frigg. One little weed, a wee little weed, hidden beneath a rock, she had overlooked. Loki, who had followed closely upon her in all her wanderings through the day, had not failed to notice this oversight of Frigg's. His wicked face shone with glee. His eyes gleamed; and as the radiant Frigg sped up the rainbow bridge, he hurried away to his home among the Frost giants to tell them of the little weed which, by and by, should work such harm to Baldur, in shutting out his life and light from Asgard and the earth.

The ages rolled on. Every one in Asgard, save Odin, had long ago thrown off the shadow of fear. "No harm can come to Baldur," they would say; and all save Odin believed it.

But a day came when Odin, looking down into the home of the dead, saw there the spirits moving about, hastening hither and thither.

"Something is happening there in the pale valley," said Odin. "They are preparing for the coming of another shade. And it must be some great one who is to come. See how great the preparation is they make."

"We prepare for the coming of Baldur," answered the shades as Odin came upon them, busy in their work. "We prepare a throne for Baldur. We prepare a throne for Baldur."

"For Baldur?" asked Odin, his heart sinking. "For Baldur!" chanted the shades. "For Baldur! Baldur cometh! Baldur cometh!"

And Odin, his godlike heart faint and sick at the thought, turned away and went slowly up the rainbow bridge.

There, in the great garden of the gods, he found Thor and Baldur and their brother Hodor playing at tests of strength. Behind Hodor, invisible, stood Loki. In his hand he held a spear.

"Shame upon you, Hodor," whispered Loki, "that you, the strong and mighty Hodor, cannot overcome Baldur in a test of strength. Baldur may be beautiful and sunny, and he is a great joy to the world; that we know. But what is he compared with Hodor for strength?"

"But the spears will not touch him. See how they glance away. Indeed it is true: light cannot be pierced," answered Hodor, good-naturedly.

"Take this spear," said Loki, quietly. "It is less clumsy than those you throw."

Hodor took it, never thinking of any harm. Alas for Baldur and Asgard and all the happy smiling earth! It was a spear tipped with the mistletoe – the one plant that Frigg had failed to find. The one plant that had not promised to do no harm to Baldur.

Quickly the spear flew through the air. One second, and Baldur the Summer Spirit, Baldur the Light of the Earth fell – dead.

"O, Asgard! Baldur is dead!" groaned Odin. "O Asgard, Asgard! Baldur is dead!"

Hodor, Thor, the gods, one and all, stood pale and white. A terrible fear settled over their faces. They shook with terror.

And even as they stood there, speechless in their grief, a twilight dimness began to fall lightly, lightly over all. The shining pavements grew less bright; the blue of the great arch overhead deepened; and in the valleys of Midgard there were long black shadows. Baldur was dead. The light had failed.

The golden age was at an end. Now, even the gods must die.

"It is Loki that has done this!" thundered Thor, seizing the great hammer in his clenched fists. "Nor will the gods of Asgard forgive this crime. No promise of his, no begging, no pleading shall save him from the punishment that belongs to him.

"O Baldur, Baldur! That I had slain the evil Loki ages upon ages ago – when he stole the hair from the glorious Sif; when he stole the necklace from the beautiful Freya; when he carried Idun and the Apples of Life away into the home of the Frost giants; when he stung the dwarf and broke short the handle of my mighty hammer. Had I slain him then, this sorrow need not have come to us. O Baldur, Baldur!"

And the whole earth shook with the grief of Thor. The skies grew black. The wind shrieked. The lightnings flashed across the sky. His tears fell in torrents down the mountain sides; trees were swept away, and the swollen rivers rushed and roared along their course.

Never, even in the memory of the gaunt old giant at the Well of Wisdom, had such a storm of wind and rain and thunder and lightning been known. The earth-people fled to the mountain caves in terror.

"It is the wrath of Thor!" cried Loki, gasping with dread. "Let me hide myself till it is over." And changing himself into a fish, he dived deep into the great seething mass of angry waters.

But Thor and Odin were close upon him. The fiery eye of Thor had caught the sparkle of its shiny coat as the great fish shot down from the mountain side into the sea. Then, too, of what use was it to hide from the great, all-seeing eye of Odin? Did he not see and hear all sights and sounds? And, more than that, did he not know all things even from the beginning?

"We will take a great net, and we will drag the sea," said Odin quietly.

Loki heard these words and trembled. He hid himself beneath the sea-weed; but so muddy were the waters that he was driven out to breathe. The great net was spread. Held by the hands of Odin and of Thor, there was no escape for Loki. Sullenly he allowed the net to close over him. There was no other way; for it stretched from shore to shore and from above the waters even to the ocean bed.

And so, at last, because it was to be, the fish held; and Loki was in the power of the angry Thor.

"Come back," commanded Odin, "to your own shape and size." Loki obeyed; and in his own form was borne to Asgard. The angry gods fell, one and all, upon him. Not one showed pity for him. They hated him. And well they might; for had he not slain Baldur, and so loosed the power of the Frost giants upon their shining city.

"Let him be bound! Let him be bound!" they cried.

"Let him be bound even as the Fenris-wolf is bound!"

"Let him be bound with iron fetters!"

"Let him be nailed to the great rocks in the sea!"

"Let a poisonous serpent hang over him; and let the serpent drop, moment by moment, through all the time to come, his burning poison upon him! Let him lie there, chained and suffering till the last great day!"

"All this shall be," thundered Thor. And thus it was that the cruel, evil-hearted, peace-destroyer Loki, suffered ages upon ages of punishment for his malice and his crime.

The gods had avenged themselves upon the cruel peace-destroyer, and he lay suffering the tortures they had put upon him.

But even this could not bring back the sunny god, the happy, cheerful, life-giving Baldur. Brage had gone, and there was no sound of music in Asgard; Idun had gone, and signs of age were again creeping over the faces of the gods; now Baldur was gone, and with him the long light and warm softness of the summer time.

"He may come back," Frigg would say; and every morning she strained her eyes to see if he had risen from behind the far-off hills with the soft light she had learned to know so well.

"Baldur is late," she would say, as the days rolled on.

But all this time, from the cold north land, the Frost giants, triumphant, were drawing near. Their chill breath was in the air. The days grew short; the nights grew long. The rivers were locked in ice. Great drifts of snow were everywhere. The sky was grey; and there were no stars. The sun shone pale and white through the dull clouds and the blinding drifts of snow. It grew bitter, bitter cold.

"The Fimbul-winter!" whispered the earth-people. "Has the Fimbul-winter come?" And Odin answered, "Yes; it is true. The Fimbul-winter, foretold by the Norns, even from the beginning of time, has come. Soon the great wolf will spring forth from the under world, and he will seize upon the sun and devour it. Then dense darkness will fall upon us; and Ragnarök – the end of all things – will be upon us."

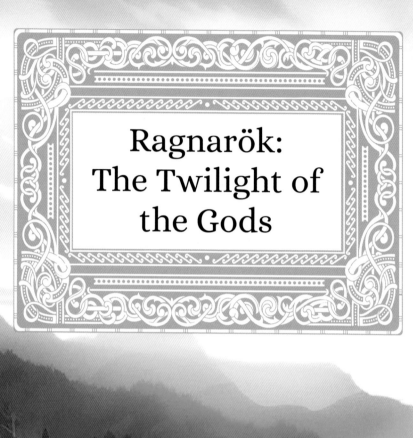

Ragnarök:
The Twilight of
the Gods

Since the day that Baldur died no one had walked in the bright halls of Broadblink – no one had even stepped through the expanded gates. Instead of undimmed brightness, a soft, luminous mist now hung over the palace of the dead Asa, and the Asyniur whispered to one another that it was haunted by wild dreams.

"I have seen them," Freya used to say; "I have seen them float in at sunset through the palace windows and the open doors; every evening I can trace their slight forms through the rosy mist; and I know that those dreams are wild and strange from the shuddering that I feel when I look at them, or if ever they glance at me."

So the Asyniur never went into Broadblink, and though the Aesir did not think much about the dreams, they never went there either.

But one day it happened that Odin stood in the opening of the palace gates at sunset. The evening was clear and calm, and he stood watching the western sky until its crimson faded into soft blue grey; then the colours of the flowers began to mix one with another – only the tall white and yellow blossoms stood out alone – the distance became more dim. It was twilight, and there was silence over the earth whilst the night and the evening drew near to one another. Then a young dream came floating through the gates into Broadblink. Her sisters were already there; but she had only just been born, and, as she passed Odin, she touched him with a light hand, and drew him along with her into the palace. She led him into the same hall in which Baldur had dreamed, and there Odin saw the night sky above him, and the broad branches of Yggdrasil swaying in the breeze. The Norns stood under the great ash; the golden threads had dropped from their fingers; and Urd and Verdandi stood one on each side of Skuld, who was still veiled. For a long time the three stood motionless, but at length Urd and Verdandi raised each a cold hand, and lifted the veil slowly from Skuld's face. Odin looked breathlessly within the veil, and the eyes of Skuld dilated as he looked, grew larger and larger, melted into one another, and, at last, expanded into boundless space.

In the midst of space lay the world, with its long shores, and vast oceans, ice mountains, and green plains; Aesirland in the midst, with Manheim all round it; then the wide sea, and, far off, the frost-bound shores of Jötunheim. Sometimes there was night and sometimes day; summer and winter gave place to one another; and Odin watched the seasons as they changed, rejoiced in the sunshine, and looked calmly over the night.

But at last, during one sunrise, a wolf came out of Jarnvid, and began to howl at the sun. The sun did not seem to heed him, but walked majestically up the sky to her mid-day point; then the wolf began to run after her, and chased her down the sky again to the low west. There the sun opened her bright eye wide, and turned round at bay; but the wolf came close up to her, and opened his mouth, and swallowed her up. The earth shuddered, and the moon rose. Another wolf was waiting for the moon with wide jaws open, and, while yet pale and young, he, too, was devoured. The earth shuddered again; it was covered with cold and darkness, while frost and snow came driving from the four corners of heaven. Winter and night, winter and night, there was now nothing but winter.

A dauntless eagle sat upon the height of the Giantess's Rock, and began to strike his harp. Then a light red cock crowed over the Bird Wood. A gold-combed cock crowed over Asgard, and over Helheim a cock of sooty red. From a long way underground Garm began to howl, and at last Fenrir broke loose from his rock-prison, and ran forth over the whole earth. Then brother contended with brother, and war had no bounds. A hard age was that.

"An axe age,
A sword age,
Shields oft cleft in twain;
A storm age,
A wolf age,
Ere the earth met its doom."

Confusion rioted in the darkness. At length Heimdall ran up Bifröst, and blew his Giallar horn, whose sound went out into all

worlds, and Yggdrasil, the mighty ash, was shaken from its root to its summit. After this Odin saw himself ride forth from Asgard to consult Mimer at the Well of Wisdom. Whilst he was there Jörmungand turned mightily in his place, and began to plough the ocean, which caused it to swell over every shore, so that the world was covered with water to the base of its high hills. Then the ship *Naglfar* was seen coming over the sea with its prow from the east, and the giant Hrym was the steersman.

All Jötunheim resounded, and the dwarfs stood moaning before their stony doors. Then heaven was cleft in twain, and a flood of light streamed down upon the dark earth. The sons of Muspell, the sons of fire, rode through the breach, and at the head of them rode the swarth

Surt, their leader, before and behind whom fire raged, and whose sword outshone the sun. He led his flaming bands from heaven to earth over Bifröst, and the tremulous bridge broke in pieces beneath their tread. Then the earth shuddered again; even giantesses stumbled; and men trod the way to Helheim in such crowds that Garm was sated with their blood, broke loose, and came up to earth to look upon the living. Confusion rioted, and Odin saw himself, at the head of all the Aesir, ride over the tops of the mountains to Vigrid, the high, wide battlefield, where the giants were already assembled, headed by Fenrir, Garm, Jörmungand, and Loki. Surtur was there, too, commanding the sons of fire, whom he had drawn up in several shining bands on a distant part of the plain.

Then the great battle began in earnest. First, Odin went forth against Fenrir, who came on, opening his enormous mouth; the lower jaw reached to the earth, the upper one to heaven, and would have reached further had there been space to admit of it. Odin and Fenrir fought for a little while only, and then Fenrir swallowed the Aesir's Father; but Vidar stepped forward, and, putting his foot on Fenrir's lower jaw, with his hand he seized the other, and rent the wolf in twain. In the meantime Tyr and Garm had been fighting until they had killed each other. Heimdall slew Loki, and Loki slew Heimdall. Frey, Beli's radiant slayer, met Surtur in battle, and was killed by him. Many terrible blows were exchanged ere Frey fell; but the Fire King's sword outshone the sun, and where was the sword of Frey? Thor went forth against Jörmungand; the strong Thunderer raised his arm – he feared no evil – he flung Miölnir at the monster serpent's head. Jörmungand leaped up a great height in the air, and fell down to the earth again without life; but a stream of venom poured forth from his nostrils as he died. Thor fell back nine paces from the strength of his own blow; he bowed his head to the earth, and was choked in the poisonous flood; so the monster serpent was killed by the strong Thunderer's hand; but in death Jörmungand slew his slayer.

Then all mankind forsook the earth, and the earth itself sank down slowly into the ocean. Water swelled over the mountains, rivers gurgled through thick trees, deep currents swept down the valleys – nothing was to be seen on the earth

but a wide flood. The stars fell from the sky, and flew about hither and thither. At last, smoky clouds drifted upward from the infinite deep, encircling the earth and the water; fire burst forth from the midst of them, red flames wrapped the world, roared through the branches of Yggdrasil, and played against heaven itself. The flood swelled, the fire raged; there was now nothing but flood and fire.

"Then," said Odin, in his dream, "I see the end of all things. The end is like the beginning, and it will now be for ever as if nothing had ever been."

But, as he spoke, the fire ceased suddenly; the clouds rolled away; a new and brighter sun looked out of heaven; and he saw arise a second time the earth from ocean. It rose slowly as it had sunk. First, the waters fell back from the tops of new hills that rose up fresh and verdant; raindrops like pearls

dripped from the freshly budding trees, and fell into the sea with a sweet sound; waterfalls splashed glittering from the high rocks; eagles flew over the mountain streams; earth arose spring-like; unsown fields bore fruit; there was no evil, and all nature smiled. Then from Memory's Forest came forth a new race of men, who spread over the whole earth, and who fed on the dew of the dawn. There was also a new city on Asgard's Hill – a city of gems; and Odin saw a new hall standing in it, fairer than the sun, and roofed with gold. Above all, the wide blue expanded, and into that fair city came Modi and Magni, Thor's two sons, holding Miölnir between them. Vali and Vidar came, and the deathless Hoenir; Baldur came up from the deep, leading his blind brother Hodor peacefully by the hand; there was no longer any strife between them. Two brothers' sons inhabited the spacious Wind-Home.

Then Odin watched how the Aesir sat on the green plain, and talked of many things. "Garm is dead," said Höd to Baldur, "and so are Loki, and Jörmungand, and Fenrir, and the world rejoices; but did our dead brothers rejoice who fell in slaying them?"

"They did, Hodor," answered Baldur; "they gave their lives willingly for the life of the world;" and, as he listened, Odin felt that this was true; for, when he looked upon that beautiful and happy age, it gave him no pain to think that he must die before it came – that, though for many, it was not for him.

By-and-by Hoenir came up to Hodor and Baldur with something glittering in his hand – something that he had found in the grass; and as he approached he said, "Behold the golden tablets, my brothers, which in the beginning of time were given to the Aesir's Father, and were lost in the Old World."

Then they all looked eagerly at the tablets, and, as they bent over them, their faces became even brighter than before.

"There is no longer any evil thing," said Odin; "not an evil sight, nor an evil sound."

But as he spoke dusky wings rose out of Niflheim, and the dark-spotted serpent, Nidhögg, came flying from the abyss, bearing dead carcasses on his wings – cold death, undying.

Then the joy of Odin was drowned in the tears that brimmed his heart, and it was as if the eternal gnawer had entered into his soul. "Is there, then, no victory over sin?" he cried. "Is there no death to Death?" And with the cry he woke. His dream had faded from him. He stood in the palace gates alone with night, and the night was dying. Long since the rosy clasp of evening had dropped from her; she had turned through darkness eastward, and looked earnestly towards dawn. It was twilight again, for the night and the morning drew near to one another. A star stood in the east – the morning star – and a coming brightness smote the heavens. Out of the light a still voice came advancing, swelling, widening, until it filled all space. "Look forth," it said, "upon the groaning earth, with all its cold, and pain, and cruelty, and death. Heroes and giants fight and kill each other; now giants fall, and heroes triumph; now heroes fall, and giants rise; they can but combat, and the earth is full of pain. Look forth, and fear not; but when the worn-out faiths of nations shall totter like old men, turn eastward, and behold the light that lighteth every man; for there is nothing dark it doth not lighten; there is nothing hard it cannot melt; there is nothing lost it will not save."

Picture credits